DYING TO
COME HOME

DYING TO COME HOME

J. B. JENKINS

Thomas Nelson Publishers
Nashville

Published in Nashville, Tennessee, by Thomas Nelson,
Inc., and distributed in Canada by Lawson Falle, Ltd.,
Cambridge, Ontario.

**Library of Congress
Cataloging-in-Publication Data**

Jenkins, Jerry B.
   [Lindsey]
   Dying to come home / by J. B. Jenkins.
     p.   cm. — (Margo mysteries : 8)
   Originally published: Lindsey. Chicago : Moody
Press, 1979.
   ISBN 0-8407-3231-7 (pbk.)
   I. Title. II. Series: Jenkins, Jerry B. Margo
mysteries : vol. 8.
PS3560.E485L56 1991
813'.54—dc20   91–18582
                           CIP

Printed in the United States of America

1 2 3 4 5 6 7 — 96 95 94 93 92 91

ONE

I should have guessed April would be a pivotal month for our detective agency when even Earl's big announcement was nearly interrupted by what would become one of our most unusual cases.

Earl Haymeyer, our boss and owner of the EH Detective Agency, had told Margo and me that he wanted to see Larry Shipman and us in his office the first thing Tuesday morning—everyone, that is, except Bonnie, our receptionist.

Had it been a Monday meeting, we'd have thought nothing of it. We three investigators met with Earl every Monday morning. He wouldn't let us schedule anything that would jeopardize it.

And we'd had a good meeting the day before. Earl may have appeared a bit preoccupied, and he'd certainly been busier than ever the past few weeks, but none of us—at least speaking for Margo and me—had any inkling of what he wanted to talk to the team about.

I didn't even worry when I noticed Bonnie all teary-eyed when I arrived. She was a wonderful woman—emotional, matronly, sixtyish—and frankly, sometimes she was moved to tears just because Earl didn't invite her to certain meetings. How was I to know he had already told her his news and that's why she was crying?

Margo and I met at the coat rack. "I had fun last night," she whispered.

I just nodded and smiled, thinking, *Me too,* and wondering if that was the best way to summarize an evening that had resulted in our setting a wedding date.

"Can we tell Earl this morning?" she asked, lifting her chin and shaking her long dark hair loose from her neck.

"Sure, and Larry too. He'll be glad to know we're giving him and Shannon a couple of weeks' head start."

Larry had fallen in love with an old friend, Shannon Perry, who had been a client of ours a few months earlier. She'd been a prime suspect in several related murders, and after we'd had a hand in clearing her, she quit her job and moved to Indiana to start over where no one knew her.

It was a pity that an innocent victim was the one who had to flee, but for some reason the distance drew Larry to her. They had developed a very close relationship during the ordeal, but not a romantic one. We teased Larry about getting next to Shannon, but he had always insisted that she was just a friend he felt sorry for.

The trouble was, when he finally did realize that he wanted to be with her all the time, she believed he was still feeling sorry for her. By then, of course, she was in the process of moving. The ensuing phone bills and Larry's trips between Chicago and Fort Wayne apparently convinced Shannon that he meant business.

By now we'd all been invited to the wedding, a small civil ceremony in Fort Wayne set for April 24. Apparently only Larry's four co-workers and a few friends and relatives on both sides would be there.

Margo wondered where Larry and Shannon would live, but Larry wasn't talking. We hardly saw him socially anymore. When he wasn't working, he was gone to see Shannon. Occasionally he'd sneak her back into Chicago and we'd join them for dinner, but their fear that someone might recognize Shannon and bring back all the bad memories was not unfounded. She did draw stares. Her picture had been in all the papers nearly every day for a long time after the murder case had been solved. Everyone knew she'd been a target, but for some reason that made them want to gawk, and she had had enough.

Earl had been in the news lately himself. The *Tribune* was playing up the governor's search for a new head of the Illinois Department of Law Enforcement. Governor James A. Hanlon and Earl went back a long way, back to when Earl had been a special investigator for him when Hanlon was the U.S. Attorney for Northern Illinois.

As part of a special recruiting task force, Earl had been interviewing law enforcement leaders from all over the country. "Silliness," he told us once. "Everyone knows Jim isn't going to take any advice to hire someone from outside the state. This guy from Florida is impressive, but why would we want someone unfamiliar with Illinois?"

Every ten days or so, Earl was called to Springfield or to the state building downtown for a confab with his cohorts on the task force. "I think I know Jim better than the rest of them, but I'm not in charge of the search committee, so I sit there and endure their gassing about finding the best man and not worrying about whether he has any interest or background in the state of Illinois."

Earl had always preached that publicity or *any* kind of visibility was the worst thing for an agency like ours. He didn't want to discourage Larry and Shannon, but he admitted that it probably was for the best that she stay in the background for a while until people forgot about the case.

Margo looked at her watch. It was a minute shy of eight-thirty. "Is he here?" she asked Bonnie, nodding toward Earl's shut door.

"Uh-huh," Bonnie said, sniffling. "He's in with Larry right now."

Margo and I instinctively turned to the coat rack again, wondering why we hadn't seen Larry's coat. Not that that would have meant anything. Earl, who's neat to the point of fastidiousness, keeps his coat in his office closet, but Larry has been known to have three or four coats on the rack without being in himself.

"He's wearing it," Bonnie said, reading our thoughts and choking up even more, apparently hoping we would ask what was wrong. We'd both learned not to ask.

"So, this is a meeting he's having with us one at a time?" Margo wondered aloud.

"No," Bonnie managed. "He still wants to see everyone—everyone but me anyway—at eight-thirty. Larry came in early on his own and wanted to see Earl. Earl's already talked to me."

I could tell she wanted us to ask her what it was all about, and it appeared Margo just might ask when Earl's door opened and he called us in. "Apparently both Larry *and* I have announcements this morning," he said.

"Well, we do too," Margo said, smiling and taking a chair Larry pulled out for her. I didn't think either Earl or Larry looked as if he wanted to hear good news, but Margo had already jumped into it.

"OK," Earl said, "you go first then." He still wasn't smiling, but it was apparent he wanted all other matters out of the way before he took the floor.

Earl and Larry had known us during the hard times, before our first engagement and during our childish split that had somehow given both of us the room and the time to mature and then get back together.

"Philip and I made it official last night," she said. "He asked me to marry him and I said yes, and if it's convenient for both our families, we'll be married Sunday, May 15."

Earl and Larry seemed genuinely pleased. "You gonna hang onto her this time, Phil?" Larry said. "You almost let her get away last time."

Earl shook my hand and embraced Margo. "So where's

that ring you could never remember to wear the last time around?" he said.

"Philip has sold that ring," she said, almost as a pronouncement. "We're going shopping for a new one tonight. Everything's new, Earl. Everything."

"There's a lot of truth to that," Earl said quietly, sitting again. He loosened his tie and rolled up his sleeves, uncharacteristically. Usually he'd look as fresh at day's end as he had in the morning.

The same could never be said of Larry. He always showed up looking like the cover of a menswear catalog, but the jacket was quick to go, then the vest buttons, then the sleeves. Then the tie would be loosened and finally shed completely. It never surprised us to see Larry heading home with his shirttail hanging out. He was most comfortable in flannel shirt and jeans, hiking boots, and an insulated vest. But Earl wouldn't let him come to work that way unless he was working on a case that required it. And guess who got the assignments for blue collar undercover work? Larry looked more like a laborer than a laborer did.

So here we sat on this Tuesday morning, Margo in a flowing, almost dressy, cream-colored dress that gathered at the waist; the usually dapper Earl starting to loosen up already; me in my usual drab, three-piece banker's outfit; and blue-collar Larry looking like an Ivy League model, his light trench coat folded on his lap.

"Larry also has some news for us this morning," Earl said.

Larry looked grim. He looked down, elbows on his knees, hands together, fingers interlocked.

"It's nothing big, really," he began, but he was having an awfully tough time speaking up and getting out what wasn't supposed to be anything big. I wondered if he wasn't about to announce that something had come up in his relationship with Shannon and that their wedding was off.

"As you know, Shannon and I will be married in about twelve days and—"

"About twelve days!" Margo mocked. "You mean *about* twelve days, five hours, thirty-one minutes, and ten seconds?"

She laughed, and Larry worked up a wan smile.

"Yeah," he said, acknowledging his preoccupation with Shannon and things marital the last few weeks. "Anyway, I don't think I can ask her to live in the Chicago area until another year or two, and I can't see commuting from Indiana, so I'm moving."

"You're moving, but you're not going to commute?"

"Right. I've taken a job as city editor of a small paper outside Fort Wayne. It's something I've always dreamed of doing. You guys all know my background; my first love has always been journalism."

"But Larry," Margo said, "you always talked about getting back into small-town newspapering when you reached your *fifties*. You're not even thirty-five yet!"

Larry still wouldn't look at her. "I know," he said. "But I don't really have a choice. And it won't be bad. It'll be fun. It's what I want. Love has had a way of changing my perspective on a lot of things."

We were speechless. It was apparent that Larry had made up his mind. And maybe it *would* be best in the long run. He was doing what he had to do and what he wanted to do for the sake of his fiancée. It was, after all, his choice.

"Are you happy about it?" I asked finally.

"Yeah, I guess I am. Yeah, I am."

"You sound ambivalent," Margo said.

"Mixed feelings I guess," he said. "I'll miss you guys."

That's what he'd really been trying to say. Larry wasn't married to detective work, though he enjoyed it. Leaving the profession wasn't going to injure him the way it would Earl, but Larry liked our little family. We were unusually close.

Margo's voice betrayed emotion. "We'll miss you too," she said. "Let's not become strangers."

"Don't worry about that," he said.

We sat in silence a few moments. "Does Bonnie know about this?" Margo asked finally. "Is that why she's crying?"

"No," Earl said, but he didn't elaborate.

"Let me tell her myself," Larry said. We all nodded, and he started to rise.

"Hey, cowboy," Earl said, "you forget who called this meeting? You're still working for me until the end of the month, aren't you?"

Larry smiled sheepishly and sat down. "Sorry, chief," he said.

"Well, I just want to say that I find myself with many reactions," Earl said. "I didn't know until Larry told me this morning, and I confess it saddens me. I think he'll be a loss to the profession.

"I have frankly been wondering how he was going to resolve his love life and his job, and I guess I just found out. You've been a top man since I first started working with you when I was at Chicago Homicide years ago, Lar. Best of luck to you."

Larry looked embarrassed.

There was still the matter of Earl's announcement, whatever it was. He'd made it clear that they both had news, but neither Margo nor I was in the mood to push him for it right then. He grew nervous, shuffling papers on his desk, straightening things, even pacing to the window and back. We stole a glance at Larry. He shrugged.

Earl pressed the palm of his left hand against his lips, looked toward the ceiling, and let his hand slide down his face to his neck and rest over the loosened knot in his tie. It was as if he had made a last ditch-effort to hold back whatever it was he was about to say.

"Well, I have some news too," he said, "and I'm afraid you

won't think it's good news." He folded his hands in front of him and took a deep breath. Before he could let it out, Bonnie's voice came over the intercom.

"Earl, someone is here to see you."

He was clearly annoyed. "Bonnie, I have no appointments this morning, and you know I'm not to be disturbed right now."

"I know, and I'm sorry, Earl, but she's pleading for an appointment."

"Will she wait a half hour or so?"

"OK, Earl. I'm putting down that you'll meet with Miss Lindsey Bemis at nine-thirty."

Earl sighed. "Thank you, Bonnie."

We smiled at Bonnie's efficiency. As a rule, she protects Earl against such intrusions, but apparently she had already heard his news and was dying to know if we had too.

"This is a difficult day for me," Earl said finally. "At eleven-thirty this morning I will be at a news conference with Jim Hanlon, where he will announce that I have accepted the position of head of the Illinois Department of Law Enforcement."

Margo gasped.

"There's no way around the fact that it means the end of this agency as we know it," Earl said. "I want to sell it and the building."

He paused to see if we had any comments or questions, but what could we say? It was unbelievable.

"I begin in Springfield on Monday, May 16. Until then we'll be finishing up the cases currently in the works. I can pay you all through the end of May, and after that I can only hope you can stay on with whoever buys the agency."

He had been talking in a businesslike monotone, but then he waxed personal and found it difficult to continue. "I have enjoyed owning and running this business more than I ever dreamed I would. I leave it only out of a loyalty to my old friend, the governor, and to the state of Illinois. It was an extremely difficult decision, and as you know, it is similar to many decisions I have made in the past, except this time I said yes.

"When Jim offered me state jobs before, none were quite so attractive and challenging. But more than that, I felt a responsibility for you, to teach you and train you in solid investigative technique and professionalism.

"That job is complete now. I have no qualms about putting any one of you in any situation by yourself. I'm confident you would do what's right."

I'm sure Larry and Margo felt as flattered as I did, but my mind was racing. Sell the agency? Who buys detective agencies? If you want to start one, don't you just do it? What's to buy? Cases? Equipment? How much would one go for? Could I buy it? What would it be like without Earl? Would any of us even want to stay on?

Somehow those questions seemed inappropriate right then, at least asking them aloud.

We had been quite some team for quite some time, and now we all were on the verge of tears. No other situation would be just like this one. There was nothing to say or ask or do. We just sat sympathizing with each other with our eyes and smiling in embarrassment at each other.

"There'll be lots to talk about as the time draws near," Earl said. "I really think Larry knew this was coming and wanted to get out of a little cleanup work." We laughed. "But he'll be gone by the first of May, you two will be married by the middle of May, and I'll be gone the next day. I have friends in similar work who might need some good people, but you'll want to wait and see who buys the agency before you make any decisions." He paused for several seconds, and when no one said anything he said, "That's it, people."

We rose slowly, reluctantly.

The ever-pragmatic Margo paused on our way out. "What

are you going to do about this appointment today, Earl? Are we, for all practical purposes, closed to new business?"

"Hm . . ." Earl said. "Let's make one last team decision. Shall we take one more case, or not?"

Larry grinned, enjoying the game. "Things are slow right now. Margo's shoplifting case is all over but the reports, and I've got only another day or so on this drug thing."

Everyone turned to me. "Philip?"

"I haven't had an actual case since you started teaching me client screening and all that, Earl. Why did you start that if you knew this was going to happen?"

"I *didn't* know. Anyway, it's been good training. What if *you* buy the agency? You'll need to know how to screen the clients."

"I know," Larry said, a gleam in his eye. "If it's a murder, we'll take it. Anything less, forget it."

"Maybe it's good you *are* getting out of this business," Margo scolded.

"But aside from that little sermonette, you're with us, Margo?" Earl said. "If it's the big M, it's a go, otherwise no?"

"Of course," she said.

TWO

"Did I say we were going ring shopping tonight?" I asked Margo at her desk.

"You said we could look."

"Yeah, but I'm still a little old-fashioned. I want to surprise you."

"So, we're not going? You're going?"

"You can come, but I don't want you to know which ring you're getting until I give it to you a few days later."

"That sounds like fun. You know, I feel a little weird getting a second diamond from you."

"I thought we were going to forget the past. Anyway, what makes you think it's gonna be a diamond? I might go to one of those classy new synthetics this time. They say even a jeweler can't tell, and I can get a big rock for a tenth of the bucks."

She wasn't buying it for a minute. She knew I'd been saving for months, eager to make this engagement better than the last. This time was for keeps, no turning back. Margo had tried to talk me out of any stone at all; she thought a simple gold ring would suffice. That showed how far she'd come, but I had to tell her how important it was to me, even if it wasn't to her. I was determined to show the depth of my love.

I knew as well as she did that the cost or size of a stone signified little apart from what was in our hearts. In a strange way, that was why I wanted it to be so special. Because this time, what was inside was full and rich and deep and mature, and we both knew it.

Of course, we had already been ring shopping during our first engagement, and I had been unable to afford the stone we both liked the best. That's always the case, of course. They show you something so far out of your reach that all it serves is to get you to come up a notch or two from where your maximum had been when you walked into the place.

But that was the first time around. The ring I bought was more than I could afford, but was much, much less expensive than the one we both wanted. This time I had decided to go for it. The ring—the one we had really always wanted—would be ready by mid-afternoon. I would pick it up on my way to Margo's for what she thought was our dinner and ring shopping date.

The excitement almost took my mind off the bomb Earl had just dropped in our laps. Almost. And by the look on Margo's face, it was apparent she was troubled about the future too. At least about part of it.

I might have forgotten my work all day had Earl not buzzed Bonnie and asked her to send in Miss Bemis and me. Lindsey Bemis had been sitting near Bonnie's desk, trying to appear patient.

It wasn't that she seemed upset that she had to wait. I could almost sense her relief that she had even gotten an appointment. Yet she sat there poring over a thick sheaf of papers that were creased and dog-eared as if they had been pored over many times before. Could she really find something there she hadn't seen before? And how many other agencies had turned down her request to investigate whatever it was she wanted investigated? I wasn't sure I wanted to know.

With her head buried in her notes, all I could see was the cascading blonde hair. She stood when she heard Earl on the intercom, and Bonnie took her coat, revealing a muted burgundy skirt and a white blouse trimmed with lace all the way to her neck.

"This is Philip Spence," Bonnie was saying as she led us past Margo's desk toward Earl's office. "He will be in on your initial meeting with Mr. Haymeyer."

Miss Bemis shifted her file folder and handbag to one arm and extended her hand, gripping mine firmly and looking me in the eye with a soft, pleasant, close-mouthed smile that I tried to interpret as confident. But Bonnie had told Earl she was pleading for an appointment. Perhaps what I took for confidence was merely persistence. Was it pain or fatigue in those pretty, green eyes?

"Nice to meet you," I said, but she said nothing.

Earl appeared a bit taken aback by her as well. I don't think he was expecting such a striking young woman. When we were seated he made a big show—at least to me—of getting up and opening one of his cabinet doors to produce a large manila envelope, a clipboard with a form attached, and a black felt-tipped pen.

I started to get up, but he waved me back down with a small gesture and came all the way around his desk to deliver the paraphernalia to me with one of his favorite looks, the one that says, "I won't embarrass you in front of our guest by lecturing you on the fact that you are supposed to bring these things to client-screening meetings, but here they are, and don't forget again."

Before Earl was even fully back behind his desk, his visitor began. "My name is Lindsey Bemis and I prefer you call me by my first name. I live in Chicago, and I work at The Bank on the Park."

Earl smiled and raised a hand. "I'm sorry Miss uh, Lindsey, but there are a few things we need to get down in a sort of order, so would you mind if I just asked you a few questions and we got our information that way?"

"Oh, sure, I'm sorry," she said quickly. She left her papers in her lap and put both hands over her face, drawing a deep breath between her fingers and letting it out slowly. "I'm just so glad to be here, actually talking with you."

Earl ignored that puzzling comment and asked for her full name, address, occupation, and all the rest. It was my job to record it on the form on the clipboard. "I'm not certain yet, if I can afford to employ you," she said, hesitating over a few questions.

"I understand that," Earl said kindly. "It's just that we get this information up front with any prospective client. We're not sure yet that we would choose to take your case either, you see?"

"Yes, OK."

"Now could you tell me the name of the bank on the park you work in?"

"That's it."

"What's it?"

"The Bank on the Park."

"Which one?"

"The one I work in."

"Right." Earl blinked slowly. "I'm missing something," he said.

"So am I," I said.

"What are you missing?"

"I'm missing the name of the bank on the park that you work in."

"No, you've got it. *The* Bank on *the* Park."

"That's the name of it?" Earl asked.

She nodded, grinning, and Earl laughed. "I guess I hadn't heard of it. Is it new?"

"A couple of years."

"I *still* haven't heard of it," I said, and the ice was broken. I toyed with the idea of telling her that we were all betting on whether her case involved a murder and that we wouldn't take it if it didn't. But there's always the possibility I would lose my bet, and then I'd really feel like a fool. Her next statement made me breathe a prayer of thanks for keeping my foot out of my mouth.

"The first thing I need to know, I guess, is whether you handle murder cases or just domestic type things."

Silence hung until Earl answered measuredly, "We have handled cases involving murder, yes."

"That's what I was told, that most private agencies handle small stuff but that EH handles anything."

"Ha, ha," I said, "yeah, that's true, we—"

"We don't handle just anything," Earl interrupted, not amused, ignoring me, and staring earnestly at Lindsey Bemis.

"Oh, no, I didn't mean to imply that. It's just that someone told me that if I couldn't get help anywhere else, I should come here."

"I could take that two ways," Earl said. "Are you scraping the bottom of the barrel?"

"No! I've done it again. I didn't mean that at all. I've not been to any other private detective agencies. But I *have* been everywhere else."

"Tell me your problem, and then tell me where else you've been for help," Earl said.

"Have you ever heard of Timothy Bemis?" Lindsey asked.

"Of course. Are you related to Tim Bemis?"

"He's my brother."

"I see."

"You wanna let me in on this, Earl?" I asked.

"You remember," he said. "The GI who murdered a clerk in the post office downtown. A couple of years ago, was it?"

"Just short of two years," Lindsey said. "And, if Timothy were guilty, I wouldn't be here." The steely core had surfaced in this soft-looking woman with the generous eyes and lips.

"But wasn't that the case that was so cut and dried?" I said. "I mean, there were more than thirty people in the place at the time of the murder, and ten or so of them identified the murderer."

Lindsey looked frustrated, stopped, reloaded, and tried again. She appealed to Earl. "Can I argue with him and start in with some of my evidence, or are we still going by your little form there?"

It was apparent to me that Earl was warming up to this feisty little woman. "Oh, uh, sure, no, go ahead. Whatever you want to say."

"Have you decided to take my case then? I mean, is the meter running from this point on?"

"No," Earl said, stifling a smile. "We haven't really heard what you want from us yet, so we'll reserve judgment on the case until then—"

"And until I've heard your price and have decided myself, right?"

"Of course. And meanwhile, feel free to argue your case with Mr. Spence while I listen. Gratis."

"Thank you," she said, almost sarcastically, holding his gaze a moment longer than necessary. This girl was some piece of work. I was hoping already that we'd take the case. We'd all enjoy this one.

She stood and used a corner of Earl's desk to spread out a couple of documents. One was from the United States government, indicating that one Timothy Meeker Bemis had been officially designated Missing In Action in Vietnam in August of 1968. The other was a report from the files of the Great Lakes Naval Training Station, indicating that the same man had turned himself in to that facility, Friday, June 5, 1981, after nearly thirteen years as an MIA.

"That story was widely publicized," Earl said, not unkindly. "The prosecution held that your brother had actually been in this country for many years before he turned himself in, and he had turned himself in just a few days after the murder if memory serves."

"That's right," she said patiently. "But Timothy says he did not escape Southeast Asia until late May of '81, arrived in Norfolk, Virginia, as a stowaway on Tuesday, June 2, and rode trains and hitchhiked to Great Lakes, arriving there on Friday, the fifth."

"Yes, I recall that," Earl said. "But if you don't mind my asking, isn't it true that the prosecution pretty thoroughly blew holes in his story? As I remember, even the ship on which he claimed to have been a stowaway had not been anywhere near where Bemis—your brother, I mean—had said he escaped."

"But Timothy was confused. He had run and swam and walked for miles and miles before he reached a coast and sneaked onto a vessel bound for the United States."

"Why didn't he identify himself to the captain and enjoy a hero's welcome?"

"He couldn't prove who he was. He looked terrible. His teeth had rotted out. He had been unable to communicate with anyone in the U.S. since the mid-seventies. He didn't know what the attitude toward him would be in this country, and he thought his only hope would be to get back to where he started."

"Great Lakes."

"Right."

"So he stole food and water, survived the trip in his ragged clothes, scrounged his way to Great Lakes, and convinced them he was who he said he was. How was he able to do that?"

"He recited his dog tag numbers, all the statistics from his original papers, mother's name, address, date of birth, and all that. They studied him, compared medical records and everything, and he checked out. They kept him there for treatment."

"Yes," Earl said. "Even after someone at Great Lakes matched his appearance with the descriptions several witnesses gave of the man who fled the post office after the explosion."

"Explosion?" I said. "I thought you said it was a murder?"

"It was," Earl said. "Someone with knowledge of the type of land mines used in Vietnam apparently threatened to blow one off if he didn't get cash or something from the postal clerk; no one heard that part. But anyway, with no other apparent provocation, Bemis—or whoever—detonated from close range a device he had strapped to his waist."

"And it didn't kill *him?*" I asked.

"No, not this type of mine," Earl said. "It was one of those lightweight, low-gauge explosives that only the closest witnesses even heard. It detonates when stepped on and is designed to send out a small shower of razor-sharp darts to destroy the feet and legs of the enemy. The darts are sprayed from the ground up and out in a small arc. Usually the device kills the person who steps on it and permanently injures one or two others in close proximity."

"But no one else was killed or hurt in the post office?" I asked.

"No," Earl said. "He had the thing strapped to his waist, top side out. When he detonated it—and it's not a loud explosion, more of a pop—all but a few of the darts hit the clerk from about four feet away. A dart embedded itself in the counter between the GI and the victim, and a couple flew over his head, one smashing a clock on the wall and another doing some other kind of damage."

"Actually there were three, besides the one that stuck in the counter," Miss Bemis said. "One hit the clock, one apparently glanced off the sprinkler system pipe and tore up several feet of acoustical ceiling, and another went directly through the dropped ceiling, hit the original ceiling, changed direction because of the weight of the tip, and dropped back through one of the new ceiling tiles, leaving just its tip exposed."

"You have done your homework, haven't you?" Earl said.

Lindsey didn't smile. She just maintained that determined look. "I know what the odds are against my convincing anyone that Timothy has a case," she said, "but I have been on this thing ever since he was sentenced, and I'm not about to give up now."

She appeared offended when Earl looked at his watch, but of course, he couldn't be late to the biggest press conference of his life.

"I'm sorry, Lindsey," he said, "but I do want you to jump right in to why you feel your brother is innocent of a charge that seems so cut and dried. The jury and the judge were very sympathetic, and had your brother's lawyer gone for an insanity plea, he probably would have had an easy time getting him sentenced to a mental institution. Even with what he had been through, the jury couldn't, in good conscience, declare him not guilty of a crime he so surely had committed. It seems I recall that a facial burn, on the forehead, made his identification rather academic for the witnesses and the jury."

"But his lawyer believed he was innocent, that he couldn't have been in Chicago at the time of the murder, and that it would have been unfair to get him off on an insanity charge when he wasn't guilty. Timothy wouldn't let him appeal, and he's never said a word in his own defense, not even to his lawyer. If I had the money, I'd have kept him on the case myself."

Earl fidgeted. "I must ask you to go ahead and get to why you feel your brother is innocent. We'll deal with his lawyer if and when we accept the case."

Lindsey dug into her files for a sketch of the murder scene and two photos that showed the clerk's body before it was removed.

Earl leaned forward in surprise. "May I see that?" he asked.

"Yes, but you can't have it. I have only a couple more, and they're in a safety deposit box."

Earl quickly turned the photo over to determine whether it was an actual Chicago Police Department photograph. It was. "Who cleared these for you?" he said, knowing that you don't just go in asking for such photos and that it would be unlikely Timothy Bemis's lawyer would let them go either.

"A sergeant, but I'm not at liberty to say exactly who. I shouldn't have even said he was a sergeant."

"Do you have the release form?"

She dug some more, producing a crumpled, soiled sheet with the initials *W.F.F.* scrawled on the appropriate line.

Earl leaned back in his chair and shook his head, sighing. "I don't believe it. Sergeant Walvoord Feinberg Festschrift wasn't even on this case. What was he doing releasing these photos to you?"

"I don't know. He was so nice. He's the one who suggested I come to you if I couldn't get help elsewhere. Have I gotten him in trouble now?"

"Why didn't *he* help you?" Earl asked.

"He did all he could. He believed me, and he let me have these pictures, didn't he?"

"That he did. And if I can determine—which I will attempt to do while I'm downtown in a little while—that Wally Festschrift is being kind to you for any reason other than that you are a lovely young lady, I'll take your case at whatever price you can afford."

"Just like that? Without even hearing my whole story?"

"Did Sergeant Festschrift hear it?"

"Yes."

"That'll be good enough for me. Can you meet with us again tomorrow morning?"

"No," she said. "I work. But any other time of the day or night."

"Late tonight?"

"Sure."

"See you here at nine. Philip, can you make it?" I started to shake my head, but Earl said, "Of course you can, and bring Margo with you."

That part would be easy.

THREE

After telling Margo that our plans would be slightly altered that night—in other words, we would have to be finished eating and shopping and everything in time to be back to the office by nine—I rode downtown with Earl.

But I didn't get to attend the press conference. "Find Wally," he said. "Tell him what's happening with me, and find out what his interest is in the Tim Bemis case."

At Homicide I was told that Festschrift was on a case. "Could you try to raise him on the radio and see if he'd call me at his convenience?" I asked.

The dispatcher did, but reluctantly. "Who do I blame this on if he don't like it?"

"I'll take the heat," I said. "Philip Spence."

"Yeah, sure ya will."

Wally phoned a few minutes later, and I stifled the urged to smirk at the dispatcher.

"Whadya got kid, another innocent victim I can help ya clear?"

"You tell me. Our client-to-be is Miss Lindsey Bemis."

"Yeah. Hey, you remember that case? The Navy MIA that was s'posed to have snuffed a post office guy with a mine?"

"Yeah, we heard all about it this morning."

"Whadya think?"

"We aren't sure yet. Earl wanted me to see what you thought."

"Got time for lunch?"

I was tempted to say, "Not your kind of lunch," but I didn't. "Sure," I said.

"Meet me at the Drake."

"The Drake? You get a raise or something?"

"Don't you read the papers, Philip? We all got raises, sergeants and up. This'll be my third time at the Drake in a week."

"And you're not tired of it? Thought you liked greasy spoons."

"Get goin' or I'll be there before you are. I'll call ahead for a reservation."

"Hey, Wally, we really don't have to eat there—"

"Don't be silly. I want to."

I beat Wally to the Drake and immediately knew it was the perfect place to bring Margo that same night. "I'm waiting for my party," I told the maître d'.

"You're not with Sergeant Festschrift, are you?"

"Uh, yeah, yes, I am."

"This way, please."

The maître d', whose discreet badge read *Francois,* deposited me at a window table for three. "Is someone else joining us?" I asked.

"No, the sergeant likes to store his wrap on the extra chair," Francois said, lips pursed and brows raised. "Doesn't like to wait upon departing. Would you care to check yours?"

"No, the chair will be fine for me, too," I said, suddenly feeling rural.

"As you wish," he said, taking it from my shoulders and folding it neatly.

"Wally's coat will smother mine, won't it?"

"Pardon, sir?"

"Sergeant Festschrift's coat. I say it will smother mine here on the chair, won't it?"

Finally aware that I was attempting humor, the maître d'
broke into a wide yet close-mouthed grin. "Sergeant Festschrift's coat, young man, could file for statehood."

Waiting for Wally, I couldn't imagine him in such an ele-
gant spot. He liked to talk loud, eat big and fast, and bustle
in and out. And his ensembles! If the maître d' thought his
coat was bad, what about those threadbare suits that barely
covered the bulging body?

As Francois reached his post, Wally Festschrift arrived and
clapped him on the back. "Hey, Frank," he bellowed, "what's
happenin'? My date here yet? Ha, ha!"

Francois began to lead the way, but Wally pulled him back
by the elbow. "Don't exert yerself, Frankie. I can find him."

Fat as ever, Wally chugged over and grabbed my hand.
"Don't git up," he said, giving me an open-palmed slap on the
face with his free hand. I was shocked when he peeled off his
coat to reveal a new suit. It actually fit. Some sensitive tailor
had had the foresight to cut the pants high on Wally's waist
and give him plenty of room for the vest and coat to be buttoned. Neither was, but both could have been, at least while
Wally was standing.

"But who stands more'n once or twice an hour in my business?" he explained. The pants had slipped from their intended perch on his waist, making the correctly hemmed
cuffs nearly cover Wally's shoes. As he sat, he hiked the trou-
sers up at the knees, exposing new shoes.

They were the same gum-soled style he had worn for
years and, not surprisingly, he still favored white socks. But
the rest of the package looked all right, all things considered.

"Does the maître d' not mind your calling him Frank?" I
asked.

Wally thought a moment. "He's never said. He didn't like
me callin' him *Fritz,* though. He told me that. Anyway, how's
Earl and what's going on?"

Before I could tell him, a waiter in a short jacket brought menus.

"Oh, we don't need menus, buddy," Wally said. "What'll ya have, Phil? I'm having the Drakeburger or whatever they call it here."

"One ground steak on toasted bun," the waiter said, writing.

"An' a coupla Cokes," Wally added.

"Two Cokes," the waiter repeated. "And your entrée?" he asked me.

"I'll have the same, but just one Coke."

"You don't care for a soft drink, so that's just one Coke?" he asked, looking at me.

"No. I *do* want a Coke, but just one."

"So that's two Cokes?"

"No," Wally said. "That's three Cokes, two for me."

"Very good, sir."

"First things first," I told Wally. "Larry's marrying Shannon the twenty-fourth of this month. Margo and I are engaged again and will be married May 15. You're invited, and—"

"Hold on! Everybody's gettin' married. Maybe I oughta get married again. My old lady—I mean, my former wife, you know . . . we're seein' each other again."

"Really? That's great! Any hope?"

"Ah, I dunno. Always hope, I guess, to listen to Margo. Margo's the one with all the hope. You too, I guess. So, is Earl gettin' married too?"

"No, in fact, Earl—"

"Don't tell me; Earl's fallen for that little blonde cutey I sent you guys' way. Am I right? I mean, I know she's too young and he prob'ly just met her. But even if you guys don't take the case, you gotta thank me for even sendin' her around. Am I right?"

I nodded, smiling. "What's the story on her, Wally? Earl

says if you are sold on her for any reason other than that she's a real looker, he'll take her case."

"No kiddin'? That's great news. Of course I'm sold on her. I wouldn't let her have police department files and pictures if I wasn't, would I? You know I wasn't on that case, but I know who was and I don't like 'im. But that's not the reason I think he fouled up the investigation. If you wanna know the truth, she convinced me. The girl, the Bemis girl, uh . . ."

"Lindsey."

"Yeah, Lindy."

"Lindsey."

"Yeah, whatever. The girl did her homework, had a good lawyer, and she convinced me."

"You talked with her lawyer?"

"Sure. He's a good young Navy guy. I'll get his name for ya. Well, she'd have it."

"We'll get the name, but what's important is that you are sure the Bemis kid is innocent."

"Oh, I think he is all right, but I have to keep my nose out of it. I could have made a real stink if I'd gotten the information sooner. But, once a judgment is handed down and the Chicago PD has played such a big role in the investigation, well, I'd be leadin' with my chin to make anything of it now."

"Wally, I know you better than that. Your justice goes both ways, doesn't it? If you know the kid is innocent, you can't let him rot in a federal penitentiary, can you?"

"'Course not. That's why I gave her a lot of advice on who to talk to and what to say and all that, and as a last ditch effort, I told her she should look up Earl. If he can't clear Bemis—and Bemis is no kid anymore, by the way; remember he was in his teens when he joined the Navy in the late sixties—well, nobody can."

"But, Wally, would you be willing to work with us on the thing—on the side, I mean?"

"Oh, I don't know," he said. "That would really be dangerous. It would have to be totally on my own time and only privately in your office, not runnin' around questioning people or anything, ya know? Is that what Earl wants?"

"No, he didn't say anything about it, but you know what he thinks of you. If he thinks you'd come, I know he'd jump at the chance to have you with us. We could sure use the help. As you know, this was made to look like a pretty open-and-shut case."

"How well I know."

Our meals were served, and Wally let out a loud guffaw, causing the waiter to turn back. "Sir?"

"What's this, a sample?" Wally said, laughing again. "If I like this I get a real one, right?"

"Sir?"

"The burger ain't bad, 'slong as I can get two. But these fries! If I can count 'em, there ain't enough. You know what I mean, pal?"

"Would you like a larger potato portion, sir?"

"Any way you wanna say it is fine with me, long as I get two of these burgers and a bigger messa fries."

"That's three ground beefs and two orders of potato?"

"No, jus' one more burger and more fries. An' if this is the size of these Cokes, I'm gonna need one more of them, too."

"Very good, and you, sir?"

"I'm fine, thank you," I said.

"I'm gonna hafta think about whether I can help you people out on this Lindy Bemis thing."

"Lindsey."

"Right."

"Think fast, because we're meeting with her tonight to tell her whether we're taking the case."

"Is there a chance you might not?"

"Not after talking with you. Your endorsement of the girl and the case is all Earl was waiting for. I'll need to tell him what makes you and Lindsey so sure Tim Bemis is innocent."

"That's a long story. Maybe I *will* try to make it tonight, but no promises of any help after that. Tell Earl I'll be there, but only this once. I could have my badge and my pension handed me on a platter over this. Which might make a better meal than I've got right here. It tastes great, though, doesn't it?"

I nodded, with my mouth full.

"Jes' not enough of it, right?" he asked.

I shrugged, my mouth still full, trying to tell him it was plenty for me.

"Any inside dope on that IDLE appointment Earl's been workin' on? Does he know who they're goin' with yet?"

"Yup. They're announcing it right now at a press conference not far from here."

"Yeah? Who'd they go with? That guy from Florida?"

"Nope."

"You know who?"

"Yeah, Earl told us."

"Can you tell me? I mean, if they're announcin' it now anyway, who'm I gonna tell?"

"Earl."

"I know Earl can tell me, an' he will, but can't you give me a little advance tip?"

"It's Earl, Wally."

"What're you sayin'?"

"I'm saying that after all the screening work and all the interviewing and comparing notes and everything, the committee recommended Earl and he took it. He just told us today. He's going to be selling the agency."

Nothing I had ever said before had stopped Wally from eating. Now he sat, a half-eaten "Drakeburger," as he called it, still on his plate. His shoulders sagged, his hands were still, his eyes unblinking. "You're serious, aren't you?" he finally managed.

He rested both chins on his huge fist and stared out the

window. He was silent for several minutes, not even noticing when the rest of his food arrived. I could almost hear the memories clicking in his head. He had a lot of questions, questions he would save for Earl.

He was subdued for the rest of the meal, though he ate everything, including some of mine.

Earl was high on the way back to Glencoe, as anyone would be who had just been the center of attention at a governor's press conference. He'd been praised by the governor himself, and the press had come prepared to ask about all the famous cases he'd been involved in.

There had been the usual speculation about whether he thought he was cut out for a job in management and administration when his forte was detective work. "I told 'em I had been in police management and administration and that much of my current work involved the same, plus training."

"I always knew you were just using us to get ahead," I teased, but his thoughts were elsewhere.

"I kinda wish now you'd been there," he said. "How was Wally?"

I thought Earl was pleased to hear that Wally would be joining us at least that evening, if not for the entire investigation, but it was hard to tell. He kept changing the subject and coming back to the press conference.

"Hey, this was the right move after all," he said, slapping me on the leg. "I think I'm gonna be glad I did this."

I hoped so, but I resisted the urge to remind him that after only a few days on the job, his honeymoon with the press would likely come to a quick end, even if his relationship with the governor didn't.

"They asked if I would take a position in Washington if Jim became president," he said. "I'd never even thought of that and told them so, but I don't think any of them bought it. Do you think Jim is presidential material? I think he could be. I mean, I really hadn't ever actually thought of it, but I think he just could be. I'd support him. I don't know if he'd even want me in Washington, but I'd go if he did. He's been good to me, always has.

"What kinda job would be available for me in a president's administration? I don't know anything about foreign affairs or anything like that."

"Head of the secret service or the FBI," I tried, just to be funny.

"Do you really think so? I don't know. 'Course I'm the only law enforcement man Jim really knows and trusts. I'd have to move, but of course, I have to move downstate now. They say Washington's pretty expensive. Have you heard that?"

"Yeah."

"But, you know a guy's gotta do what a guy's gotta do. I don't think I could even think of turning down a request from the president of the United States, could you? When's the next election, anyway? I don't know what Jim's plans are. Guess I'll be finding out soon enough."

I just smiled. Earl had a way of returning to reality in a matter of minutes sometimes. This time might take longer, but I assumed he would be back to his level-headed self by nine o'clock.

FOUR

Larry had the next two days off and was going to see you-know-who, so he didn't have to endure Earl's stratospheric rambling all afternoon. I was the only one in the office who got much done, because I'd heard it all before.

When Margo left for the day, I nearly knocked Bonnie over on my way out to the jewelry store a few miles north.

It was pushing five when I picked up Margo. "You look as excited as I am," she said.

"I'm glad you're excited," I said, hoping my secret wasn't obvious. She had changed into a tweed suit over a cowl-necked sweater. "Lovely," I said.

"Where we going?" she asked as I merged onto the Edens.

"You'll see."

"Oh, goodie. A surprise." She sat close and rested her head on my shoulder. "But Philip," she said, suddenly straightening up, "if we're going all the way downtown, we might not make it back before the jeweler closes."

"Don't worry about that," I said. "Anyway, I thought you didn't want a diamond."

Silence. I looked at her, trying to keep from smiling. I couldn't. Neither could she.

"You're the one who's got me all psyched up over a diamond," she said. "As long as your heart is set on it, I'm going to enjoy it."

"And your heart *isn't* set on it?"

"It is now," she admitted. "I love you, Philip."

"Of course you do; you can't help yourself."

She punched me.

We parked underground and walked hand in hand toward the Drake. When she spotted it from a few blocks away, she looked at me quizzically but didn't say anything. I pretended not to notice. We crossed the street, but just before I should have headed toward the door, I pulled her to the right as if we were going past it. Then I turned back.

"Oh, Philip," she said, realizing what I was doing. "Not the Drake! It's perfect." She hugged me right there on the sidewalk.

"Francois told me you'd take care of me," I whispered to the evening maître d' while pressing a large bill into his hand.

"Yes sir. Mr. Spence, is it?"

I nodded.

"And this is your intended, Miss Franklin?"

Margo smiled.

"Right this way, please."

Everything was perfect. The table, the flowers—compliments of the house—the view, the service, the food. "And the company," Margo said.

"Can't argue with that," I said. "Margo, you're so special."

Before dessert, Margo asked if I minded talking a little business.

"It's up to you, Babe. This is your night."

"*Our* night," she corrected.

"Then sure, let's talk business."

"What can you tell me about this woman we're going to be talking to tonight?"

"Lindsey Bemis is her name," I said, and I told Margo as much of the story as I had been able to piece together.

Margo remembered the case and the attendant publicity, assuming, as we had, that there couldn't be too great a possibility that the jury had been wrong. "Still, we've learned to trust old Wally, haven't we?" she said.

"That's for sure. This could be an interesting swan song."

"Oh, don't say that, sweetheart," she said. "I'm not ready to give up our work, even if Larry and Earl are. Are you?"

"Hardly. Though I do have the illustrating to fall back on."

"Yeah, and I could go back to waiting tables."

We laughed.

"Seriously, though," she said, "this is a strange day with so much sadness and happiness mixed. I'm going to miss Larry and Earl and the agency and even the office."

"I know what you mean. I'm glad we've got other things to think about for a little while here."

She reached across the table with her left hand and covered my right. "OK, let's think and talk about us. We've got a wedding to plan."

The maître d' approached with a note of congratulations from the management.

"How sweet," Margo said. "Thank you."

We chatted for another hour or so before Margo started glancing at her watch every few moments. "Are you sure they have evening hours, Philip?" she asked.

"Sure. Hey, you've come a long way from not wanting a diamond to being so eager to pick one out."

"And you love it," she said.

"You got that one right," I said.

"Even if they *are* open late, we have to allow enough time to get back to the office by nine."

"I know, Babe, I know. C'mon, relax."

She smiled self-consciously. "I'm sorry," she whispered.

We pulled up in front of the jeweler's store in Highland Park just before eight o'clock, and it appeared they were preparing to close. "Oh, Philip," she said, reaching for the door handle, "we have to hurry."

"Whoa, hold it," I said. "At least for today I get to be a male chauvinist, don't I?"

"OK, but hurry!"

I jogged around to her side, digging deep into my coat pocket for the small square box. But instead of opening her door, I signaled her to open her window.

"Philip," she said, exasperated as she rolled it down.

"Why don't we forget the shopping and just settle for this?" I said.

She appeared unable to speak as she opened the crinkly bag and pulled out the wrapped box. A tiny card slipped into her lap. As I looked in, elbows resting at the top of the lowered window, she read, "Because He first loved us. You'll always have me. Philip."

She smiled up at me, her eyes moist. "I love you," she whispered.

I put my hand behind her head as she unwrapped the box. She hesitated before prying open the springed lid. Light from a street lamp danced off the big marquise stone when she raised the top. "Oh, sweetheart," she said softly. "It's too beautiful." She drew my hand to her face and pressed my fingers to her lips. I leaned in to kiss her, and her tears ran down my cheek.

I took her to her apartment and waited in the car while she changed and freshened up for our late meeting. She skipped back out in slacks and a sweater under a light jacket, her ring shining. "It's almost too big," she said. "Maybe I shouldn't wear it in public or someone will steal it."

"I told you before, it's fake," I said.

She ignored me and held it up to the light. It shone like fire. "And I'm the Easter bunny," she said.

On our way to the office, she said, "It's not fair, you know."

"What's that?"

"I wanted to give you my gift when you gave me yours.

You said it wouldn't be for a few days, so I'm not ready with mine yet."

"What gift?" I said. "The boys get to give the gifts in this game. Not the girls."

She laughed. "Well, anyway, we gotta set another date, because in a few days I'm giving you a gift and it's got to be special."

"Fair enough," I said, wondering what in the world she had up her sleeve now. "You decide when and where and ask me out. Then you can give *me* a gift."

We arrived at the office before anyone else, so we sat talking in the car. "You know, Philip, we can't wait any longer with Earl."

"You mean spiritually?"

"Uh-huh. He's so close, to the point where he's tried to tell Wally what it's all about. And though he and Wally came to church with us that one time, and he came back another two times, we're letting Earl slip through our fingers."

"Through *our* fingers?"

"You know what I mean. I know God won't let him slip if he's meant to become a Christian. But I just think we'd better not let up now, especially with him leaving in thirty-four days."

"You're counting the days before Earl leaves?"

"No, silly. I'm counting the days before our wedding. He leaves the next day, remember?"

A car swung into the lot. "It's Lindsey Bemis," I said.

We walked over to her car and I introduced her to Margo, "my fiancée."

"How nice," she said. "When's the big day?"

"Today was one big day," Margo said, showing her ring. "But the real big day is May 15."

I unlocked the door, and we went upstairs to the offices. "Are you the vice-president or something, or does everyone have a key to the office?"

"No, it's just that both Earl and I live in this building. Earl owns it, actually. We all have keys to the office, but he and I, as tenants, also have keys to the outside door."

Lindsey's look made me wonder if I had told her more than she'd asked. Margo puttered at her desk while I watched out the window for Earl and Wally. From the reflection in the glass I could see Lindsey moseying around the room, reading the plaques and letters on the wall.

"Mr. Haymeyer is a pretty accomplished man," she said.

"That's right," Margo said, rising and moving closer to her. Lindsey moved away. I could tell Margo wasn't sure yet if Lindsey didn't want to be approached or if it was just co-incidence, but when Margo moved toward her again, Lindsey moved again. So Margo went back to her desk.

"He was named head of IDLE today," I said, "the Illinois Department of Law Enforcement."

"Is that so?" she said, not realizing what it would mean to the EH Detective Agency or her own case if it went past May 15. "Is that good?"

"Good for the state," Margo said. "Not good for us."

"Why is it not good for you?" Lindsey asked, coming up behind me.

I turned, surprised that she had asked me when Margo had broached the subject. Margo stared at me from over Lindsey's shoulder, apparently wondering the same.

I told Lindsey the ramifications of Earl's appointment. She pursed her lips and cocked her head and moved away again. She was certainly one beautiful girl. But puzzling. How could she have something against Margo without even having gotten to know her? It didn't seem possible, but it would have seemed even more implausible if she could have something against Margo *after* she got to know her.

Earl and Wally happened to pull in at the same time. They shook hands and embraced, then trotted up the stairs to-gether, Earl gliding, Wally lumbering. At the top, Wally puffed and sweated for several minutes, forcing him to just nod and wave when greeted by each one in the room. He knew us all from somewhere or another, yet he was unable to speak until he caught his breath.

"We can have our meeting right here," Earl said, sitting on the edge of my desk and pointing us to various chairs and desktops. "I know we're all tired, but we owe it to Miss Bemis—"

"Lindsey, please," Lindsey said.

"Lindsey. Excuse me. We owe it to Lindsey to hear her whole story and then make a reasoned decision about accepting her case."

"You're gonna accept her case, I can tell you that," Wally said, still breathless. "I only wish I could help officially."

Lindsey spread out her documents again and told a bizarre story of Timothy Meeker Bemis who had just turned nineteen and had been in Vietnam one year when captured by the Viet Cong. "How old were you at that time, Lindsey?" I asked.

"Oh, let's see, I was born in 1958, so I would have been about ten. I was nine when Timothy went into the service, and we corresponded frequently."

"How frequently was frequently?"

"At least twice a week from the time he enlisted until he was assigned to 'Nam. Then I wrote at least once a week. But I heard from him only every two or three weeks—very old letters referring to my letters from weeks before. I learned quickly about military mail and wartime red tape."

"How would you explain this close relationship between a nine-year-old girl and her eighteen- or nineteen-year-old brother?" Margo wanted to know. "Did you know then how unusual that was?"

"No, I didn't. I do now, of course. But we were always close. We were just far enough apart in age that I couldn't get in his hair, and he tolerated me—thought I was cute. He was in high school when I started kindergarten, so he really was something special to me. I thought he could do anything, and he could. I didn't have any other brothers or sisters. He was it. My father died shortly after I was born, so Timothy had to play both roles in my life: dad and big brother. My mother had to work, of course, but Timothy was very responsible."

"Did he help support the family?" Earl asked.

"He had a trade. Sheet metal. I think he studied it in shop at high school half days and then worked in a local shop the rest of the day. Something like that. Made a little money; not much. Was a good, responsible kid. Just after my father died, according to my mother, Timothy got in with a bad crowd for a while, but when he got over his grief and anger, she was able to get through to him and persuade him that his father would have wanted him to take responsibility, make something of his life, and all that. Of course, back then he was too young to get a real job, but he started doing yardwork, delivering papers, that kind of thing."

"So, he was a basically good kid after that," Earl said. "That doesn't jibe, of course, with the picture the prosecution painted of him at the trial. They said he'd always been a troublemaker, and that even though he didn't have a bad high school record, he was a laborer type, whatever that meant—as if there is something intrinsically criminal about someone who makes his money with his hands rather than with his head. Anyway, the service record was not all that good."

"I know that," Lindsey said, not defensively. "And apparently they were not exaggerating some of the trouble he got into after he'd been in 'Nam a while. Some of my letters from him show that he had had it. Now I can see that it was battle fatigue, and his lawyer saw the same thing. He wanted to come home . . . Here, look at this."

She pulled an old letter from an airmail envelope and spread it carefully before her upside down so we could all read it as we crowded around. "This paragraph here, especially," she said. "Don't mind his spelling—"

It read:

Maybe I was wrong about Talia, but I had met the girl on R & R and I felt so guilty that I thought I should tell her. I know now of course that this girl meant nothing to me except that I was lonely and tired and angry and wanted to come home and knew that I couldn't. I'm afraid the only way to get Talia back is to come home and explane it to her, because she hasn't ansered my letters for months. I can't blame her, but this is driving me crazy. Listen, kid, I know this might sound off the subjict, but don't ever do any *dope, I mean any dope. There are guys around here who just started on grass because of the fear and bordom and now they're doing cocane and everything else. It's a dead end and there going to ruine themselfs for life. I don't know what I'm going to do about getting home, but don't be surprised if you see me walking up the road one day.*

"So, you think he tried to go AWOL?" Earl asked.

"I know he did," Lindsey said. "They caught him, and he wrote to me from some sort of a mobile detention camp where they hold guys who are to be shipped back to federal prisons or be dishonorably discharged for desertion or whatever. He wrote this:

Well, I blew it. I didn't make it. I'm not sure how I feel about it. You know I cared about the country and everything and that's why I joined, but it just seems like I was drivven to get home and I couldn't think of any other way. One of the shrinks here tells me he thinks he can get me off on a disonerable and I shoutdn't have to do time, but no promises. I should be home in three weeks.

"Well," Lindsey said, weary from painful memories, "I didn't hear from him for three months. I started writing Washington and my congressman and everything, and the next thing I heard, he was declared missing in action. Well, you know what I thought then."

"No," Earl said, "don't assume we know anything. What did you think then?"

"I thought the Navy had set him up or killed him or left him somewhere to rot. I mean, why should they treat a deserter any better, even if it was the situation—I mean, the war and the personal thing and everything—that made a good guy make a mistake?"

"I'd hate to think that would happen," Earl said. "I don't want to be naive, but a lot of troublemakers *were* shipped back, and most were pardoned or at least given some sort of discharge that won't ruin them for life. The government was at least that understanding."

"Oh, I know, and I found out that that wasn't what happened to Timothy. He somehow got a letter smuggled out, and to this day I don't know who sent it to me. It came by way of New York. Here it is."

Dear Linny,
I have no way of knowing if this will ever get to you. A guy and me who are escapeing have traded letters and whichever one of us makes it will try to get them to the U.S. I guess if you get this and I don't show up, you can figure I got caught, but let me tell you something. Unless you hear for sure that I got killed, don't believe it. Tell Talia I still love her and that I will be coming back. I already decided if I get caught, I won't do anything stupid because as much as I want to escape, I also want to stay alive so I'll take the torchure and will stick it out as long as I can. I will always think it's hillareous that the Cong capsured a bunch of disonerables.

"How did it happen that you didn't give up hope if you didn't hear from him again for more than ten years?"

"Somewhere during that time, I got this list from Washington of MIAs that the government had reason to believe were still alive and in custody over there. His name was on it. Frankly, I *had* given up. Then I went at it like a banshee, making a fool of myself with every military and government agency in Illinois and the U.S. Then the last delivery of prisoners was made and Timothy was not one of them, even though his name was on the list. The government told me that he had apparently not understood that he was going home with friends, and that he 'escaped' from the U.S. contingency and was never found. He was still officially listed as missing until he turned himself in at Great Lakes."

"The key question remains, Lindsey. How can you be sure Timothy did not pull the post office job?"

"I can't believe he had the strength or the brain to do it, and I can't believe, either, that he had the time. He has a vague memory of begging for money on the street in Norfolk and being directed to some mission where he scrounged up some used clothes. But he was so sick and wasted from his ordeal, he couldn't have stopped off in Chicago to kill somebody. For one thing, he didn't have a motive."

"But if he was mentally unstable, and by this time he had to have been, he wouldn't have needed a motive."

"Yes, I'm afraid he *was* unstable by that time, because I heard from him one more time before I knew he was in the States. This letter came several years before he arrived and was sent by a guy he had met, apparently a part of this group that was to fly home together.

"The guy sent a note with it."

Dear Miss Bemis,
 Your brother insisted that I send this letter to you in case he escaped. I tried to tell him that he was free now and didn't need to escape, and that he could deliver the thing to you himself in a few days, but he made me take it. I guess I should have known he wasn't quite right, but none of us really thought he would make a run for it now that we were all safe. But when we

*mustered for roll call the morning of the flight, he was gone. I
sure hope he makes it home.*

And she carefully spread on the desk the last missive from
her brother.

FIVE

In a weak, squiggly line that looked like the work of an elderly arthritic, we read:

Lin:
I'll try 1 more time to get out of here. My teeth are gone. I have sores. I don't think you want to see me like this. You wouldn't recognize me except my scar. But I'll never give up. Don't you ether. Talia's probly married by now. I think Mom's dead. Is Mom dead. I think she's dead. Sometime I think I'm dead, but I no your still wating for me. I'm alive.

"I didn't realize he had the scar on his forehead before he went into the service," Earl said. "I guess I thought that was a 'Nam related injury."

"No, it was from a splash of solder when he was learning that in school, I think when he was a junior. But anyway, the scary thing was that he was right on all the things in his letter. Talia was married, our mother had died, and I was still waiting for him, believing he was alive. I don't mind telling you, though, I thought he'd made a fatal mistake by thinking he had to escape from his own troop plane home. I was really angry that the one who had delivered this letter didn't tell someone or try harder to talk him out of it. He needed help, not messages delivered."

She had grown more and more emotional and then broke down. Margo moved to comfort her, but she stiffened.

"Is there a reason you're uncomfortable with me?" Margo asked.

Lindsey hid her face and shook her head. "My mother had long, dark brown hair," she said. "Even up to the day she died, she never had to color her hair. Her pictures, from when she was younger, look a lot like you."

"Don't resist me," Margo said. "Don't pull away from me just because I remind you of someone you love."

"I loved her all right, but she sure had bad timing. If she could have held on a few more years, she'd have gotten to see Timothy again, as she always dreamed. You have no idea the number of times we gave him up for dead. Then another jolt would come, another shred of information giving us that frustrating, elusive hope. Of course, I could read between the lines when sometimes Mother couldn't. She didn't sense any of the drug-related problems, I think, as I did. All she knew was that Timothy was rotting somewhere in Southeast Asia, ravaged by loneliness, disease, homesickness, or who knows what. There were times when I wondered if it might not be better if he did die over there. He wouldn't be dying in peace, but at least his wretched existence would end. Then I'd pray he would return so we, or at least I, could nurture him back to health, physically and mentally. He was such a good person before he left, and I still maintain that anything and everything that has happened to him has been because of that crazy war and the pressures on the boys."

Margo whispered, "You really grew up during the long wait for him, didn't you?"

Lindsey nodded.

Earl fidgeted. "I don't want to push you, Lindsey," he said, "but Tim Bemis's past and the tough things that happened to him along the way don't prove that he didn't get off the train on his way to Great Lakes and commit this murder. Wasn't there a record of some smaller crimes he pulled in Virginia?"

Lindsey composed herself. "Yes. He stole some money, but he wasn't armed. Both times he was able to distract gas station owners and then break into their cash registers. He got less than one hundred dollars total in the two thefts. He just took the money and ran, and the station owners didn't identify him until his picture was broadcast all over the country in connection with the post office murder. He doesn't even deny those crimes. He had to have money, and his panhandling wasn't working because he was so pitiful looking by then that people avoided him."

"Show Earl the postcards, Lindsey," Wally said. "The ones from the various points on his way to Great Lakes."

Lindsey dug through her folder and produced postcards, all apparently stolen from the same gas station in Virginia, which Timothy had sent her from selected towns during his train ride. A few fellow passengers had been located by his attorney, but their testimonies that he had indeed been on that train didn't impress the jury, and everyone still maintained that Bemis would have had time to pull the job in Chicago and then take the train to Great Lakes.

Everyone, that is, except Lindsey and her lawyer and Wally Festschrift.

Earl unintentionally silenced us by rifling through his briefcase. We waited expectantly. "I have here a couple of clippings from news accounts of the trial," he said.

"Nothing I don't have," Lindsey said. "You can bet on that." And she produced her own clippings file.

"This one in particular," Earl said, unfolding it. "The prosecution refers to several crimes committed in the southwest U.S., where your brother was positively identified. And these were drug-related busts."

"I know, and they were all during the years he claims he was still in 'Nam. So, it makes him look bad, and since no one on the ship, the one he stowed away on, remembers him or will admit to it, it makes him out a liar. It's as if he's trying to cover his tracks and say he wasn't even in this country when those were committed."

"Have you ever thought of this, Lindsey?" Earl said, pausing to think and pursing his lips. "Is it possible your brother used you to try to clear himself? I mean, those letters you received always came through a third party and didn't have Vietnam stamps or paper purchased or manufactured in Southeast Asia. Could he have been sending those from inside the States here, trying to establish that he was still overseas when he was, in fact, here living a life of crime in the drug underworld?"

Lindsey smiled slightly. "I have thought of that," she said. "And there are times when I've actually allowed myself to consider the possibility that it was true. I know my value judgments of a brother that I hadn't seen for more than ten years would be outdated. I can't guarantee that he's of the same character as when I knew him. I believe he had done drugs in 'Nam, and I believe his mental capacity was diminished by his experience there. But no, I don't see him capable of pulling that off, morally or mentally. In fact, it's the evidence from those crimes in the Southwest that convinces me he's innocent in Chicago."

"Me too," Wally said.

"I don't get it," Earl said.

"Do you have the clipping from the *Tribune* that shows the picture supposedly taken of Timothy in a Phoenix police station?"

"No."

"Let me show you."

Only a year or so old, the newspaper was brittle. It showed a pathetically thin, dreamy-eyed Timothy Bemis, half asleep, half sneering at the camera.

"Are you saying this isn't your brother?" Earl asked. "It sure looks like him. Scar and all."

"Scar and more is the problem, Mr. Haymeyer. This man has teeth. My brother has no teeth, I mean *no* teeth. And he hadn't had teeth at least since he got that note out to me before the evacuation that should have brought him home."

"What does that tell you, Earl?" Wally asked, a twinkle in his eye.

"Obviously you think somebody's setting him up or using his identity to hide their own."

"More'n that, Chief," Wally said. "We can even narrow it down, can't we? We know it had to be someone who knew pretty much what Tim Bemis looked like, but who knew him when he had teeth. That puts it somewhere between his junior year of high school and the time of his last letter to Lindsey here when he tells her he has no teeth."

"Can you be sure that was his writing?" Earl said, suddenly suspicious of everything.

"Oh, yes. It was a mess, but it was Timothy's writing. I've even had that checked out by a graphoanalyst."

"Why doesn't that surprise me?" Earl said.

"It can't be used in court, but would you like to see the report?"

"No, I'll take your word for it. You're quite a researcher, and persistent. Have you been able to maintain any sense of humor or any enthusiasm for life in all of this?"

"It hasn't been easy," she said, allowing a smile of appreciation for the concern. "But I'm living to clear my brother's name. I just feel he's been through enough and has more than paid for his wrongdoing in 'Nam and even his small thefts on his way to Great Lakes. If he didn't commit this murder, and I'm convinced that he didn't, he should be freed to get himself back together."

Earl turned his attention to Wally. "If you don't mind my saying so, Sergeant, I don't see enough here yet to convince an old pro like you that Miss Bemis has a solid case. What am I missing?"

"What you're missing, Chief, is something that a guy who was just named to an important post should have seen as quickly as I did when I studied this material."

"Touché. So, I'll bite. What?"

"Lindsey's guess," Wally said, "and mine too. Uh, you don't mind if I run with this, do you, honey?"

"Not at all, please."

"Her guess and mine is that somebody in one of these prison camps, sometime before the last evac that Bemis should have been on, escaped and made it back to the States with Timothy's identity. It had to be someone who was aware of the scar but unaware of the dental problem."

Earl was warming to the idea. "You're convinced that this," he said, pointing to the picture from her newspaper clipping, "is not your brother?"

"At first I wasn't sure. I had seen him only a couple of times in more than a decade, and I have to tell you, the first time I saw him he had to convince me he was himself."

"How do you mean?"

"Well, he had to weigh almost a hundred pounds less than when he went off to the Navy. He was a big kid. In fact, he just barely made the weight limit. If I remember right, they told him he ought to take off ten pounds just to be sure, so he wouldn't get drubbed out the first day. He weighed right around two hundred and twenty-five pounds.

"Now, when he sent me a picture after six weeks of boot camp, or basic training, or whatever they call it in the Navy, I was amazed. He was still big, had lost only about ten pounds, and his features were real defined. His eyes were deep and dark. He looked good and handsome and trim. He looked hard. He had that same look in every picture I ever received from him, and the last one . . . Let me see if I have it here. Yes, see? It shows him only a little more drawn.

Maybe he'd lost another ten pounds. But he's five-foot eleven and a half. And I'd guess that here he weighed around two hundred, wouldn't you?"

"Not much less than that," Earl said, comparing the faded color print with the newspaper clipping. "Yeah, this guy who was busted in Phoenix can't weigh much more than a hundred and a quarter soaking wet, even if he was just under six foot. Looks wasted."

"Well, that's what I thought about Timothy when I first saw him. The scar on his forehead was the only thing I recognized, so he was right about that in his letter, too. But his hair was stringy and thinning terribly. Before, he hadn't had a receding hairline, of course, but now what was left of his hair was graying. He'd had average brown hair and green eyes. But, it was his teeth and his weight that shocked me most. I hate to admit it, but even when he trembled and called me by name at Great Lakes, I asked him a bunch of questions to determine if he was really Timothy."

"What'd you ask him?" I asked.

"Oh, my mother's maiden name, her birthdate and the place."

"That would have been on his records. An impostor would have been able to come up with that."

"I know. I also asked him what he used to call me when I was little and what were my favorite toy and animal." Lindsey had a faraway look and seemed to be remembering, not just her conversation with her long lost brother, but also her childhood with a big brother who gave her more attention than most would have.

"He called me Poopsie. I don't know why. It made me giggle, and he liked that. And my favorite toy was an old rag doll I never wanted to give up. He couldn't remember its name, but he convinced me when he came up with the name I gave my imaginary Palomino, *Star Diamond*. I hugged him so hard I almost hurt him.

"He said, 'You don't have to touch me. I've seen myself in the mirror. I know.' It just made me cry and cry. I told him I didn't care, that my prayers had been answered and just seeing him alive made him beautiful to me. But he thought I was lying. He was just the core of what he had been, teeth missing, eyes vacant, skinny, weak, listless. His lips trembled when he knew I believed he was Timothy, but he had no more tears. I don't know if he was all cried out or if something, that soft emotional center of him, had been one of the casualties of the years.

"He told me briefly how he had come from his last prison camp, which he decided was an unofficial torture center for unaccounted for GIs, made it to the coast, stowed away, and wound up in Norfolk. He even told me he had stolen money to make the train trip to Great Lakes, thinking he would get help from the Navy before he called me. He wasn't surprised when I confirmed his fears about Mom. Anyway, I've rambled and it's late, but I'm telling you without a doubt, the man in the picture from this paper, the one who committed all the crimes in the Southwest, is not my brother. At first it was hard to tell; if you've seen one wasted body you've seen 'em all, but this one has teeth. My brother has teeth now that they've arrested the infection and were able to work on him. Even with teeth, I can't get the two of them to look alike in my mind. There's something else that convinces me these are two different people."

She was having trouble speaking again. We all leaned forward, and Margo put her hand on Lindsey's arm. "What is it?" she asked softly. "I know this is hard, but we need everything we can get to help you."

"Well, no matter what Timothy had been through, there was something about my second visit with him that convinced me he was the same person. I mean, he wanted to make over the fact that I had grown up to be a real woman and all that, and I wanted to get started on rehabilitating him.

The arrest had already been made on the post office thing, of course, but I was so sure there was nothing to it that I refused to even think about the fact that he would be sent to a federal penitentiary as soon as he was healthy. But no matter what I brought him to eat or what I advised or how I encouraged him, he kept bringing the conversation back to me. He was amazed that I had kept the faith, had "kept a candle in the window"—that was the way he said it. He said thinking of me all those years was all that kept him going, and he just prayed that I would somehow have gotten his notes and would never give up. He asked me if I had ever wavered. I lied and said no, but he knew I was pretending. He smiled weakly and said, 'You always were a lousy liar. I gave up hope, so you must have, too.'

"Mr. Haymeyer, you can call it sentiment or family ties or whatever you like, but my brother didn't kill anybody. He wasn't in that post office once in his life. He's never been to the Southwest either, as far as I know. And I'd like you to help me prove it."

Earl leaned back and took a deep breath, looking around the room at the rest of us. Margo was teary-eyed, trying to signal him with a look that we should take the case. I was stunned by the story, wanting to believe it but still full of questions, wondering why Bemis had never been very vehement in his own defense.

Wally was giving Earl one of his knowing looks, as if to say he knew the new director of the Illinois Department of Law Enforcement had been enchanted to death by this girl and would take the case for free if necessary.

"For some reason," Earl said, "your brother never denied the southwest U.S. crimes. But, if your timetable is right, he couldn't have been there. What do you make of that?"

"I don't know. He's told me, of course, that he doesn't remember much about the trip from Norfolk, but he does know he was nowhere else from the time the ship docked to the time he reached Great Lakes. He figures, I think, that there is no way they can link him to the crimes elsewhere, and since they threw them out and only tried him for murder, he never cared much one way or the other."

"But he does deny having committed them?"

"Oh, yes. To me, anyway."

"And what does he say about the post office murder?"

"That gets complicated. His lawyer first wanted to plead temporary insanity and throw Timothy on the mercy of the court because his mental capacity was so limited he literally didn't know himself if he had committed the crime. But at the last minute, something inside Timothy told him that I was right."

"That *you* were right?"

"I'd been badgering him to plead not guilty. I knew he was innocent."

"But didn't the judge say, during sentencing . . ."

"I know. That if Timothy had pleaded not guilty by reason of insanity or if he had even pleaded guilty, the judge would have shown mercy and gotten him treatment and all the rest. If you're wondering if I feel guilty about pushing him into his not guilty plea, yes, I do. When I look ahead and realize that the odds are slim that I will ever convince anyone who can do any good that Timothy is not guilty, I feel terrible and can only hope that Timothy knows my intentions were good. I hate to settle for the lesser of two evils, but maybe that's what we should have done."

"Why didn't his lawyer appeal?"

"He wanted to, but Timothy said no. He said prison in the U.S. was so much better than in 'Nam that if he could get some medical attention and decent food and if I could visit him regularly, he'd rather just take his sentence. I worked hard on him, but he was just tired. He'd had it, and now I'm beginning to know how he feels. His lawyer told me who to go to and what to look for, and I've done my best. But I can't cut through the red tape. I hate to even admit that. But a year after the sentencing, here I am, wondering if I can employ a private detective agency with a good reputation on a cashier's salary."

Earl folded his arms and stood, stepping close to Lindsey and towering over her. "You're certain you want this looked into, even if it means we find he's guilty."

She started to protest, but decided against it and nodded.

"You know what you said about the odds being against your ever convincing anyone who could do any good?"

"Uh-huh."

"Well, you just did it. Maybe I'm foolish to think I can cut through any more red tape than you have, but I promise you this: it's the kind of challenge I like. I might not be as convinced yet as everyone else here is that Tim Bemis is innocent, but if he is, we'll get him out of prison for you."

"Oh, thank you, Mr. Haymeyer. You don't know how much—"

"Let me say one more thing," Earl said. "If we do find that the decision of the court was accurate, I'm going to have to level with you on that, too."

"I'm not worried about that. I just want you to know how much—"

"You'd better let him tell you how much," Wally quipped, and we all laughed.

"There's no way you can afford half our rate, so we'll work out something. I should add one stipulation, however."

Lindsey looked worried.

"Why don't you turn on the Lindsey Bemis charm and persistence and work on Sergeant Festschrift here. If we're going to take this case at a cut-rate fee, we're going to need all the free help we can get."

Lindsey smiled. "That's the kind of challenge *I* like," she said. Wally covered his eyes with his hand.

SIX

By the end of the following week, Larry Shipman had completed his final assignment for the EH Detective Agency. He had tracked down a brilliant young Navy lawyer named Harold Freeman and discovered that Freeman was not only eager to get back to civilian life and his own law practice, but he was also willing to take on the Bemis case again, and would do it gratis.

With all his files copied—with the permission of the U.S. Navy, which could have stalled that process for weeks had it not been for Earl and Wally's friends in high places—we assembled a mini-command headquarters for the case in the front office of the agency. All our other cases had wound down, and we were enjoying the teamwork, the way it had been when Earl first formed the agency.

It somehow kept our minds off the fact that this would be our last case together. We knew Earl was busy trying to sell the building and the business, but the showing of the premises was handled by his real estate man, and we were hardly aware of it.

Margo and I talked a lot about what we'd do, and Earl arranged interviews for us with friends of his in the business. Things were tight, though we were both getting a few nibbles. For a while it appeared that we would be unable to work together in another agency because they had policies against such things, which became apparent as soon as we told them we would be married within the month.

Margo was still insisting on the date that she would initiate when she could give me my wedding gift. We'd been terribly busy, but we finally decided on Sunday night, the twenty-fourth of April, when we would return to Chicago from Fort Wayne after the Shipman-Perry wedding.

Being a bit old-fashioned (sexist, according to Margo), I was a little uncomfortable with her asking if I was available, and would I care to join her for dinner and a drive that night, but it would be fun.

The afternoon of Friday, April 22, I was in the bank depositing my check when I ran into an old friend of ours, Hilary Brice, a lawyer. She had represented Margo's interest in her mother's estate.

"Hilary?"

"Philip! Philip, how are you? It's, uh, a surprise to see you. I mean, it's good to see you. How's everything at the agency? I hear Earl is selling."

"Yeah, right. Where'd you hear that? Have you seen Margo? She'd love to see you again. We'll have to get together."

"Oh, well, I heard it around. You know, your boss is becoming quite the media darling. We'll see how long that lasts when the press mood changes."

Something was different about Hilary. She had never been one for small talk. She seemed nervous or troubled, almost as if she wished she hadn't run into me and wanted to get moving. I was about to make it easy for her when Margo emerged from one of the side offices. She approached Hilary quickly and then noticed me.

"Philip! Hilary! What are you doing here? It's good to see you. Both!"

We all laughed.

"Margo," I said. "I've got your check. You didn't need to come to the bank, did you?"

"I guess not," she said, "but I wanted to ask about canceling my checking account when we open our joint one and—oh, it's nothing we have to bore Hilary with. How've you been?"

"Fine," Hilary said. "And you?"

"Fine."

"Well, this is scintillating," I said, smiling, "but I'd better get in the line here before they close. You need a ride, Margo?"

"No, I drove."

I shrugged and got in line. I thought we had discussed coming to the bank together one day the following week to get everything in order for our joint accounts. "Good to see you again, Hilary. Let's all get together one of these days."

"Right. Bye."

If I hadn't known better, I would have thought they arrived and left together, but it didn't compute.

I asked Margo about it on the way to Indiana, but she maintained she was as surprised as I was to see Hilary. "We really do have to get together with her soon," she said. "And we have to talk turkey with Earl, too."

"I know. I can't imagine his turning down every invitation to church lately. He used to go with us now and then, but now he doesn't and he never really seems to have a good excuse. I'd quit asking if I thought it irritated him and he was trying to avoid us, but it really doesn't appear that way to me."

"Me either," she said. "I got the impression he would have gone with us this morning if we hadn't all remembered at the same time that we'd be driving to Indiana. I'm glad we drove alone. It's good for Bonnie to have some time with Earl."

"Yeah. He was a little puzzled, though. I don't know what he thinks we're up to, coming alone."

"Well, I don't think he wanted to get back as quickly as we do. But I have a hot date tonight."

"You do?" I said. "Does that mean *our* date is off?"

She shot me a double take and shook her head. "Incurable," she said.

The Shipman wedding was sort of a sad affair. They were happy enough, but they left God out of the ceremony, the way He was left out of their lives. It was a civil ceremony and was over in minutes. No music. No prayer. No acknowledgment of anything remotely religious. The family on both sides was nervous and uncomfortable in front of strangers.

All the way back to Chicago, Margo seemed depressed by it all. "It gave me a lot of ideas for our wedding," she said.

"I thought you were all set already."

"I was, but this just makes me more determined to make it clear to everyone what we're all about. I mean what you and I are about, and what the wedding is all about. Then if our marriage is as beautiful as our wedding, we can't complain."

"What a nice thought," I said. "Like a wedding card."

She lay her head on my shoulder and seemed to sleep for a hundred miles or so. When she stirred, she said, "Will we make it back in time for church?"

"Um-hm."

"Good."

I had joined Margo's church after a couple of years in a larger one. I loved the services at the small church, especially Sunday nights. Lots of singing and people telling what God was doing in their lives. Of course, there was always a sermon. That night's was on the armor of God and was called "Put it on, put it all on."

Sometimes this guy's titles were better than his sermons, but not this night. I wished Earl could have been there to hear it, and I wondered where he was. He had been so close, even to the point of having talked at length to Wally Festschrift about God. Margo and I will never forget the night Earl told us that and asked advice on what to say next. We had asked him where he stood on the whole thing, and he admitted that he was still considering it. Meanwhile, however, he knew it was something Wally needed and was checking back with us to make sure it was as simple as we had always made it sound.

He was finding it hard to believe that it's just a matter of acknowledging your sin and believing in Christ to forgive them and take charge of your life. We told Earl that yes, that was basically it, the way we had been saying all along. When we doubted he was listening, he hustled back to tell Wally some more.

The best I could figure, Wally—who had come to church with us once himself—was still considering all the ramifications of becoming a Christian. Just thinking about it had already made a difference in his relationship with his former wife and his kids.

Wally we would have more contact with; Earl was heading for Springfield in three weeks. We were feeling the pressure with Earl. We didn't want him to get away and get down there where he wouldn't have any spiritual input, no one to care, and too much to think about in his job to have time to continue considering God in his life.

Margo had pushed Earl hard to commit to joining us at church on Sunday, May 1, and he had said he wanted to talk to us about it. Oh, the hours we spent speculating about that. Was he, once and for all, going to ask us how to become a Christian? Was there more he needed to know? Was he afraid God would expect more from him than he had to offer? Did he think God would not let him take this big, new, exciting job offer?

Or was he going to kindly tell us to back off and quit

asking, and couldn't we take a hint. We just didn't know. We kept praying for him and assuming the latter, worrying more than we should have. Even on Margo's "date" after church, while she was leading up to the big gift—which was not too well hidden on the floor of the backseat—it seemed all we could talk about was what Earl wanted to talk to us about.

"We'll find out in the morning," I said.

"Yeah. And won't it seem strange without Larry in the Monday morning meeting?"

"Won't it seem strange not to *have* a Monday morning meeting?" I said. "What's to meet about? We've only got the one case."

"Right, but Earl's going to make the final assignments on this one. I wonder if we'll get to work on something together."

"Without Larry around anymore? Fat chance. Anyway, we never have before. If I were Earl, I wouldn't put us together either. Hey, where we goin' to eat? I'm hungry and eager for my present. You gonna open the door for me and everything, this being your date and all?" I just couldn't help teasing her.

"Sit there and wait for me, and you'll go hungry," she said. Her smile after a shot like that is as beautiful a smile as she has. I was going to love being married to this woman.

We had a lovely, late leisurely dinner at a French restaurant in Highwood, which she paid for. Then she drove me back to my apartment at the office. As we sat in the little parking lot with only a street light at the corner providing any illumination, she arched over the back of the seat and grabbed the box from the floor.

"To Mr. Spence from the soon-to-be Mrs. Spence," the card read. I was fighting to hide a grin, loving this.

I untied the bright green ribbon on the package, which was the size of a shoe box. When I got the paper off, I realized that's what it was, a shoe box. I wondered if she had somehow decided it appropriate to present me with a pair of shoes as a wedding gift. Or maybe she had picked out the ones she wanted me to wear with my tux. That would have been all right, I guess. I didn't know what to expect. A watch or something similar is what I had guessed when I allowed myself to think about it. Margo didn't make a great deal of money, but she had so looked forward to this night that I figured she had saved up, or cooked up, something special.

"Shoes?" I said, lifting the lid. Sure enough, there was the white tissue paper you find in a shoe box, but the box was too light to really have shoes in it. I dug down through the paper and found nothing. I looked at her, puzzled but trying to appear amused.

"It's there, Philip. Keep digging."

At the bottom of the box, under all the paper, was an envelope. A handmade card? That would be perfect. A clue that would lead me to another clue and then eventually to the gift? Not like Margo, I guessed.

I opened the envelope. Two folded pieces of paper; I couldn't guess what either was in the darkness. I opened a tiny white note and held it toward the street light. "With all my love forever, Margo."

I leaned over and kissed her, but she was nervous, preoccupied. I unfolded the other sheet and squinted at it. It appeared to be a check. She turned the inside light on. It *was* a check, a cashier's check, made out to me in the amount of $894,656.

Margo was chattering, but I wasn't hearing her. Later I would realize what she was saying: "When you saw Hilary and me at the bank, I thought I'd blown it. This check isn't really negotiable, of course, because it would be foolish to have that kind of money out of the account even for an instant. So what it really does is represent the transaction I made Friday with Hilary's help. It was transferred to your account—what will be our account when we're married, and we were able to do it without losing any of the interest."

"What is this, some kind of a joke?" I said, not amused.

Her expectant smile froze and faded. "Everything I have is yours, that's all," she said. "I don't want to own anything that you aren't a part of."

"What're you talking about?" I said. "Are you serious?"

She tried her smile again, but I wasn't showing any interest.

"What is this?" I demanded again.

"It's the settlement, sweetheart. We thought it was going to take years, but Hilary and her former boss, Amos Chakaris, were able to get it done. Mother's house, the furnishings, the antiques, the stocks and bonds, everything was liquidated, and even after all the lawyers' fees and everything, it netted one-point-one million. I gave a hundred and ten thousand to our church, anonymously. That should get that Christian education building and kids' clubs facility built, and no one will ever guess where that kind of money came from. Then I gave about ninety thousand to Daddy because he needs it and because Mother really should have left him something anyway. He tried not to take it, but he finally agreed. I think he was grateful."

"Margo, you can't be serious."

"I am, darling, and I hope you're happy. I've felt terribly guilty about deciding on that tithe without consulting you, but I didn't want to spoil the surprise, and I didn't think it would be fair to be collecting the interest on that amount when it belonged to the Lord. You don't mind, do you?"

"Mind? Mind what you do with your own money? No, I don't mind. I have no say about it, except I'll say this. I can't accept this. I don't want it. Do you have any idea what this kind of money means to a person like me? It means zip. It means something for nothing, gravy. It means bad luck. It means I could never be a true North Shore type like you. I don't see how you can take this in stride when I choke to death on it. Forget it. I don't want it, and I won't take it. I don't know what you're going to do with it, but I don't want any part of it."

"Philip!" she moaned. "I don't understand. You had to know we'd have to deal with the settlement someday."

"I guess I thought I could put off worrying about it. Ah, forget it!" And I left the check and the note and the paper and the box and the wrapping and the ribbon and Margo in the car while I stomped in the door, up the stairs, down the hall, and into my apartment.

I slammed the door, kicked my shoes off against the wall, and went to the window. I stared down at Margo in her car. Now what should I do? I was so mad, yet I didn't understand my own reaction. What had insulted me so? And how could I talk that way to the girl I loved?

Should I run back down and talk to her? Nah. What would I say? But what had I done to her? What would she think? I started toward my shoes but heard her start the engine. I went back to the window and saw her pull slowly away.

Now what?

I put my shoes on and trudged out into the night. Clouds hit the moon, and the wind whipped at my trench coat. I walked fast, trying to burn off the anger, the offense. The worst part of it was, I didn't understand it myself. What had I said? Did I mean it?

What was she trying to say with such a gift? Surely she hadn't intended to show me up or put me behind an eight ball. That was her idea of generosity? It hurt me, and though I knew it wasn't intentional, it made me angry at her for some reason. Was it her naiveté? How could she have known the impact it would have on me? She couldn't. Even *I* was surprised, so she couldn't have known.

I walked so fast I hardly realized where I was going. I got out onto Glencoe Road and just kept moving, hands jammed deep into my pants pockets, coat unbuttoned and flapping in the cold wind behind me. My hair flew, and I wore a scowl so deep I could almost see it from the inside. I was mad, and I couldn't even articulate why in my own mind.

I walked and walked and walked, wondering what I was supposed to do about the next morning. Maybe there was something to these crazy policies about not letting spouses work in the same office. What was a couple supposed to do when they had problems?

Did this jeopardize our plans? No, not if she could be talked into getting rid of the money somehow. Did it change my feelings toward her? I didn't know. I didn't love her any less, but something had definitely changed. I hadn't felt this way toward her for months, since before our split.

Was this another childish episode that I was responsible for? I hoped not. No, this feeling was so deep and real that anyone in his right mind would have to feel the same. What a way to end a nice day!

When I realized I was coming up on the sign for the Lake Front Park just north of Winnetka, I stopped dead and turned around. *What am I doing?* I thought. *It'll take me forever to get back unless I hitchhike!*

I decided that was a stupid idea and just started walking back, at about half the speed that had carried me this far. I wanted to get the whole thing settled in my mind. But I couldn't. What had bothered me about it so? It drove me so nuts even thinking about it that I wanted to burst. What I needed to do was somehow chew out Margo, show her how wrong it had been. That would have made me feel better, but what about her? Was I being fair? Couldn't I allow her some remnant of naiveté from her childhood?

When I finally returned home, I was hot despite the cold wind. I flopped on my bed, still in my clothes, and prayed for drowsiness. Not a chance. I wondered if Margo had tried to call while I was out. Would she worry that I wasn't there? Would she come looking for me? Would she call again? And if she did, was I in the mood to talk to her? No. If the phone rang, maybe I shouldn't answer it. But I've never been good at ignoring phones, doorbells, or unopened mail.

Should I call her? Definitely not right now. One thing was clear in this jumble of angry thoughts: I had not handled the situation with Margo well at all. I would have to rectify that eventually, but now certainly was not the time. The later it got, the more difficult it would be for me to have the mental facility to even think the thing through.

I was too keyed up to sleep and too tired to think clearly. I lay staring at the ceiling for hours, trying to sleep or think, one or the other, and failing to do either. I finally fell into a fitful slumber at about 5 A.M. and woke up with a start at 7:00, realizing that I had not set my alarm and that I had less than half an hour to get to the big meeting with Earl.

And this wasn't business. This was at Earl's request to talk about why he hadn't been accepting our invitations to church for the past several Sundays. Margo and I should be prayerfully working in tandem on this one. How were we supposed to have any positive impact on him in this condition, basically not talking?

The one thing I hoped for was that Margo would be her usual levelheaded self, even if I wasn't. She had a way of rising above petty problems and prioritizing the important ones, the spiritual ones.

But I had hurt her. I had seen it in her eyes as I was leaving the car. I knew as well as she did that Earl's spiritual life was more important than our problem, but that kind of money wasn't minor, either.

As I shaved I decided that if it had been two million dollars, Earl and what we said to him today was more important. I prayed that I could postpone my other worries, significant as they might be, long enough to be and do whatever it was God wanted of me that morning. I figured Margo would be in at least that frame of mind. Maybe later I'd find the fortitude to take this estate thing to God too.

I started down the hall on automatic. Ooh, I was tired.

SEVEN

I didn't know what to expect from Margo, and I would have been happier to have slipped in either before or after her without being noticed. But as I neared the glass double doors outside our offices, she reached the top of the stairs from outside. There was no avoiding her.

I knew I had to say something. I stopped, opened the door for her and started to speak, but she just reached up with both hands and drew my head down to hers, planting a big smacker on my lips. She pulled away ever so slightly but held on with her hands and whispered, "Whatever our problem is, we'll work it out, because we're meant to be."

And with that she breezed past me with a thanks for the open door, hung up her coat, and sat at her desk. I stared at her, overwhelmed. She winked at me. I shook my head. Earl poked his head out of his office in his usual way and invited us in.

Margo maneuvered so she was behind me as we entered, and she squeezed my elbow with both hands. I was dazed. How could she do it? How could she tell me with a few coy moves that we were going to survive this?

We were both shocked to see the Reverend Charles Grassley of my former church. He rose as we entered and greeted us by name. The first thing that flashed through my fatigued brain was that he somehow got Earl's permission to beg me to come back to his church.

But we had talked about my reasons for joining the church

Margo belonged to. We had agreed it was better for her and for our relationship. Maybe there was a family emergency, I had lost a loved one or something—

"I asked Reverend Grassley to join us this morning, because he's played an important part in this. Not as important as the two of you, of course, but important nonetheless.

"You two have been wondering why I keep turning down your requests to come to church with you. Flat out, the reason is that I have my own church. I appreciated and often thought of Reverend Grassley's sermon the one time you took me there, and while I like your church a lot too, Margo, I just felt drawn back to this one.

"You know, from the beginning—at least from the beginning of the time I started listening to you, Philip, instead of just tolerating you, or not tolerating you as the case may be—I've considered this, um, conversion business more of a private affair than you do."

I started to protest, but he raised a hand and continued. "I know you don't think you see it that way, and I also have appreciated your concern—both of you—in the way you talked with me about it. When I felt pushed or pressured, I let you know and you backed off. But you never gave up.

"The big thing was, and you probably know this already, that I sensed you cared. It was more that than anything you said because I couldn't understand much of it. I guess it all became clearer to me when I tried to tell Wally Festschrift about it. But anyway, the thing you couldn't have known as I have for several months—in fact, almost a year—was that I was on the right track.

"I knew that what you were saying and what you were, uh, showing or displaying or whatever, was true. I knew I was intended to be a Christian, to believe in Christ. It was just a matter of time, and when I sensed your urgency about it, I thought I'd better get serious.

"You'd given me a lot to read and think about, and I kept

telling you that it was a decision only I could make. You agreed, but I could tell that frustrated you because you didn't know whether to keep the pressure on and push me because of how important this is, or whether you should just leave it up to God to handle me. No doubt, you thought I would drift from the influence if you didn't keep an eye on me."

I smiled a self-conscious smile. Earl has always had a way of cutting right through to the heart of something. I shot a glance at Margo, who was already fighting tears. Reverend Grassley sat smiling benignly with his overcoat and hat in his lap.

"Well, anyway, the pastor has a breakfast he has to get to, but I wanted him here when I told you. He said the most important thing, after one becomes a Christian, is to tell someone else. I couldn't think of anyone I'd rather tell."

"Tell us more," Margo said. "I want to know when, how, everything."

"Well, it wasn't anything dramatic like your story, Margo. I just decided that the time had come and that everything made sense and that this was what God wanted, and what I wanted. So one night after church, I made an appointment with the pastor and he prayed with me. It's been about three weeks."

Earl looked to the pastor who nodded, smiling. "I really didn't need to be here, did I, Earl? I think you thought this would be much more difficult."

"I did, you're right. I thought it would be embarrassing, but by the looks on your faces, you've made it easier. I'm glad you came anyway, Pastor."

"Me too," he said. "You want to tell them about Springfield?"

"Oh, yeah. Pastor Grassley has a colleague who pastors a church down there, a good church, the kind he's confident to let me attend—" they both laughed. "So I'll be checking that out the first thing when I get down there."

Margo, still fighting tears, took a deep breath and raised

her eyes to the ceiling. "I can hardly believe this," she said. "I know I should; it's what we've been praying for forever, but . . ."

We all laughed. "You know, Margo, I tried to hint at it one time," Earl said. "The day we announced Larry and I are leaving. You missed it."

"You're kidding. What did you say?"

"You had said something about Philip's selling your first engagement ring because you wanted everything to be different this time. You said everything was new, and I said, 'There's a lot of truth to that.' "

"I remember your saying that, Earl, but I thought you just meant all the changes in the agency. You're a better detective than I am. I never would have put that together."

"I probably wouldn't have, either," Earl admitted. "It *was* a bit obscure."

The pastor spoke. "I wonder, Earl, if you'd like to have prayer with your brother and sister here before we all start our workdays?"

"That would be great," Earl said. "If there's one thing that both puzzles me and excites me at the same time about this thing, it's the new lingo, the terminology. A lot of it goes right past me, but I do feel like your brother now."

We stood and held hands all around, and Pastor Grassley prayed. "Lord, we praise you for salvation. For forgiveness of sins. For new life. We praise you for the gift of your Son who gives us this new life, abundant life, eternal life. And we pray that today and every day we might be shown worthy to be called by Your name and to be part of Your family. Protect our brother. Give him the strength, the power, the encouragement, and the people of God that he'll need to grow in his new faith. We pray in the name of Jesus Christ. Amen."

Margo had let go of my hand during the prayer to wipe away her tears, and I was glad she did because I needed a free hand, too. With her hand still covering her mouth, she said,

"I cannot believe we just had a prayer with Earl Haymeyer." Earl laughed and embraced us.

At an extended lunch, Margo and I tried to talk about the previous night. She could tell I hadn't slept. "I didn't sleep well either," she said. "Philip, I don't understand. All I wanted to do was tell you, to show you, to make real that everything I have is yours. I don't want anything apart from you. And I thought maybe even this would allow you to buy Earl's building or even the business."

"I'm not ready to run a detective agency, Margo, but that's not even the point. I wish I knew why I reacted like I did, and I hope you know I didn't intend to hurt you."

"I know that, sweetheart, but you acted as if I hurt you. And apparently I did, but you have to know that I didn't mean to."

"I do."

"But now tell me why it bothers you so."

"I don't know."

"If you wanted to give me a gift like that, I'd be thrilled."

"But I'll never be able to give you a gift like that. Maybe that's the problem. Maybe it threatens me. Maybe it's silly chauvinism again."

Margo toyed with her food. "How serious is it, Philip? Is it something you'll get over and can accept, or is it so strong that I should think about doing something else with the money?"

"If you'd asked me last night, I could have told you easily. Right now I don't think I could ever accept it, and yes, I think you should do something else with it."

"But if I own it, if it's mine and I invest it or take the interest from it, won't that get between us too? I mean, you wouldn't really feel like you were providing for me if I had that kind of security tucked away, would you, Philip?"

"No, but it would be the same if we just decide the money

is mine or ours and not yours. I'll still know where it came from. It'll always be your money. I guess I want you to get rid of it before we get married."

She looked stunned. "I don't know what to think," she said. "Are you making it a prerequisite? Are you saying that you'll marry me if I'm a girl with no means, but that having money somehow makes me a different person? One you can't live with the rest of your life?"

"I know how that sounds, Margo, but I can't help it. I guess if I'd met you and you were a rich girl, you probably would have thrown me over immediately upon finding out that I work for a living."

"That's a prejudicial statement against the type of people I grew up with. You know if God hadn't intervened in my life, I might have lived like that myself, even without my mother leaving her estate to me. Not all wealthy people are shallow and judge others by their possessions. And I sure hope you know that I don't."

I was frustrated. I would like to have thought that Margo would be different, that she would be one who could marry a commoner. But I had never had to think about it before. When I first met her and learned she had wealthy parents, I wasn't in love with her. And by the time I was in love with her, her means were gone. Now they were back and it bothered me, so maybe I was the problem, not her. I didn't like to think about that.

"How would you react if I gave you a gift like that?" I asked her.

"I'd appreciate it, I think."

"Well, I appreciate you, Margo, and I appreciate the fact that you wanted to give me the biggest and best gift you had. If it represents you and all that you have, then I'm flattered. But can you see how it could emasculate me?"

"I don't know. I guess so."

"And you say you'd accept a gift like that from me?"

"Sure."

"Then you've got it."

"What are you saying?"

"I'm saying I accept your gift. And, now that it's mine, I'm giving it to you. I do have the right to do anything I want to with it, don't I? Or were there strings attached after all?"

"You know better than that. You're just confusing me, Philip. You know it's rude to turn down a gift or try to give it back."

"It can also be rude to give an inappropriate gift."

I had hurt her again. I could see it. I knew it when those words came out of my mouth. "I'm sorry, Margo. I didn't mean that the way it sounded."

"I know, but it hurt anyway. Is that the bottom line with this? It was an inappropriate gift?"

"I hate to say it because I know your intent was pure, but yes, I guess that's where I am on it. And I really do want you to accept it back."

"But Philip, it has to come *back* with no strings too. That means I can just turn around and give it to you again."

"But you won't because you know how I feel about it. You don't want me to have to accept an inappropriate gift. I know you don't see it that way, so please, take it back and know that I love you more than ever."

"What does that have to do with this?"

"It has everything to do with this, Margo. I love you for giving me all of yourself and all your possessions, and I love you because you love me. And I am overwhelmed with my love for you. The last thing in the world I want to do is hurt you, yet I know that's what I've done. I was hurt, too, but that was my problem. I want you to forgive me for any pain I've caused you, and I need you to believe that I never want to hurt you, no matter what I do or say."

"Well, the same goes for me, Philip. And you still want me

to take back my gift, even if I don't fully understand why it bothers you so?"

"Exactly. And someday you will."

"Will what?"

"Understand."

"Will you at least tell me what I'm supposed to do with it? If I'd wanted it in the first place, I'd have kept it. And from what you've been saying, you don't want me to do anything with it that would make life easier for you or for me."

"Like what?"

"Like investing it or buying Earl's business, or whatever. Buying a house?"

"No."

"Putting it in trust for our children?"

"Admirable, but don't you want to provide for our children by the work of our own hands? Maybe I'm selfish or blind, but I don't want something handed to me for my family. I want to be able to do my part."

Margo sat thinking for a long time. "I'm looking forward to the day when I understand this, Philip. Something tells me that your passion for the subject somehow lends credibility to your view. I don't feel quite so convinced of my opinion." She chuckled. "Don't think that will always make our arguments easy. Passion for your point of view won't always convince me. It hardly does now. But I'll accept the gift back and will pray about what to do with it. And I'll let you know as soon as I can so it won't threaten our wedding plans."

"Nothing would have done that," I said.

"Not even if I had not accepted the money back?"

"Not even that, but you might not have appreciated what I probably would have decided to do with it. Of course, if it weren't for my freedom to give it back to you, I never would have accepted it in the first place."

"Somehow, I still find this painful, Philip."

"I know, and I'm sorry. I really am. No one would believe this, would they?"

"I hardly do myself. You know what Hilary's advice was in the first place?"

"Hm."

"She said if I was bound and determined to give it to you, I should at least have a document that provides for it to return to me upon the dissolution of our marriage."

"Oh, really? As if that's a foregone conclusion."

"Of course. Her hypothesis was that even if we started with a strong relationship, which she agrees we have, the money would do us in eventually."

"Hey, maybe she has more insight than we know."

"I know. It almost did us in before we got started."

A waitress was moving from table to table with a chalkboard bearing a phone message. "What a neat idea," Margo said. "That way there's no paging or bothering everyone unnecessarily."

I nodded as she came by. The board read: "Philip, call Earl."

"Yeah, Earl, it's Philip, what's up?"

"I need you and Margo at the office right away. Can you make it?"

"Of course."

"I wonder what's happening with Lindsey or Timothy Bemis," Margo said in the car.

"What makes you say that?"

"It's the only case we have left, Philip. What else could it be?"

"Who knows? It could be something with Larry and Shannon."

"But what?"

"I'm only guessing, love. Just like you were."

EIGHT

As if Earl couldn't even wait until we jogged up the stairs to the office, he was waiting in the parking lot when we arrived. He sat on the hood of a car I didn't recognize, and Wally Festschrift leaned against Earl's car. They introduced us to Lieutenant Harold Freeman, a stocky young man in a Navy dress uniform.

I expected Earl to lead the way to the office, but he was content to have our meeting right there. "Have you seen the paper today?" We shook our heads. "I hadn't either," he said. "Look at this."

He unfolded the first section of the *Tribune,* and everyone grabbed a corner to keep it from blowing off the hood of the car. "'Airtight' Bemis case resurrected; Homicide Cop's Involvement Probed."

Earl read:

> While the detective agency owned and run by Earl Haymeyer, slated to assume control of the Illinois Department of Law Enforcement May 16, is reportedly dredging up the Timothy Bemis murder case, the Chicago Police Department's internal investigation unit is probing the involvement in the case of veteran Homicide Detective Sergeant Walvoord F. Festschrift.
>
> Haymeyer, former Chicago Homicide Chief and special investigator in the U.S. Attorney's office when Governor James A. Hanlon held that office, has been unavailable for comment, but

police department sources speculate that the Bemis case will be Haymeyer's last before he closes his EH Detective Agency to avoid conflict of interest complications related to his new post.

Sergeant Festschrift, a colorful and often visible homicide investigator, is a veteran police officer with more than thirty years' experience, more than two thirds of that in his current position. Festschrift has reportedly passed up numerous opportunities for promotion because he apparently enjoys his area of expertise.

Festschrift's involvement in the newly revived Bemis case was brought to light by one of Festschrift's colleagues, Homicide Detective Sergeant Robert Richard. Richard allegedly tipped off the Internal Affairs Division that Festschrift had authorized the release of confidential police department records and photos to Lindsey Bemis, twenty-five, the younger sister of convicted murderer Timothy Bemis.

According to sources close to the investigation, Richard is convinced that Festschrift is aiding in the private reopening of the Bemis case in a jealousy-motivated effort to discredit Richard.

Their disagreements have boiled over into public charges and countercharges before, once resulting in two-day suspensions for each. Richard told the *Tribune* he fears no such eventuality in this case, "because this time I've got him dead to rights. Just because he wasn't on this case and it generated a little notoriety, he wants in on the limelight."

The police department has announced that Festschrift, who has been unavailable for comment, is under investigation for unauthorized release of police department records and photos and for engaging in private investigative and consultative work on his own time without departmental approval.

Timothy Bemis, a Navy Vietnam MIA, was convicted last year of the 1981 slaying of U.S. postal worker Lloyd Cavenaugh. . . .

"And it goes on," Earl said.

"Bob Richard is a scoundrel," Wally said. "He doesn't give a rip about justice. All he cares about is Bob Richard."

"Were you wrong in releasing the stuff to Lindsey, Wally?" Margo asked.

"We don't think so," Freeman said. "Oh, he may have violated some departmental policy, but it's minor and would certainly not take precedence over new evidence in a murder case."

"Could Wally be thrown off the force for that?" I asked.

"Not without a fight," Freeman said. "He might be wise to sit still for a wrist slapping, but there's no way he should lose tenure or pension or benefits or salary over a minor infraction of departmental rules when his overall intent was that justice be served."

"But what does it mean for his working with us on this case?" Margo said.

"Well, he hadn't actually begun working with you on it. He had served in a consultative role, but without compensation. So I don't think they have anything there. However, they cannot preclude his gainful employment during a suspension that could result in loss of income. So, ironically, he's freer now to help you than he was a day or so ago."

Wally flashed a mischievous grin. "Don't you just love people who can talk like that?" he said.

Earl was still troubled. "This is the kind of publicity I don't need. Not for my sake, but for Jim's. All he needs is for his new department head to be in the middle of some kind of conflict of interest or nose thumbing of police procedure. Got any advice for me on that one, wonder boy?"

Freeman was not offended by the remark, but rather seemed to be hiding a grin. He did indeed have some advice for Haymeyer. "You're an old friend of the governor, are you not?" Earl nodded. "Why not give him a call and explain the whole issue?"

Earl trotted up the stairs.

"So, Wally," I said, "what's your next move?"

"I dunno. If I get any heat from the Chicago PD on the strength of that, that Richard, I'll be walking. Maybe I'll be walking anyway. I've had enough red tape over the years. I like Earl's kind of work."

"You go into private investigating and you can count me in," I said.

"Me too," Margo said.

"Even if it meant workin' for an old slob like me who'll have to live with the stigma of 'leaving the force under fire'?"

After about twenty minutes, we heard a tap from inside the upstairs window. Earl was still on the phone but was signaling us to come up. Freeman folded up the paper.

Earl was pacing around the office, carrying the phone from my desk and dragging the cord behind him. "Uh-huh, uh-huh, right Jim," he kept saying. "Yeah, well, I've not gotten any real nibbles, and I've been wondering what I was gonna do in the event I don't sell. Well, hey, OK, you'll get back to me then, huh? Thanks a lot, Jim. Thanks a lot."

We sat waiting expectantly as Earl traced the trail of cord and got the phone situated back on my desk. Then he looked at us self-consciously and sat in my chair, putting his hands behind his head and leaning back. "Whew!"

"So what already, Earl?" Margo said.

"Jim knows Richard, you know? And he knows the Chicago PD inside and out, too. Seems Richard was close to being probed himself by Jim Hanlon a few years before I joined the Attorney's office. Nothing Jim can hang over his head now, but enough that Jim is confident that Richard won't want to do battle with the governor.

"Anyway, Jim likes what we've got on the Bemis thing already. He doesn't want to have to go the pardon route unless he has to. Much rather get an overturned conviction, which I think we all agree would be better." We all nodded. "He says if Wally gets too much heat on the interdepartmental thing, that I ought to think about asking him to take over my agency while I'm in government. I asked him if I could get away with that, and he said sure, as long as I have on file an affidavit that stipulates that I will in no way associate myself with the agency other than as an absentee owner. I can't do anything that would send business its way or in any way favor it, financially or otherwise. But that's easy."

"You mean have me run the EH Detective Agency?" Wally said, incredulous.

Earl didn't respond. He just grinned at Wally. The fat man stood and began pacing, rubbing his hand over his face and head. "Well, I don't know."

"Actually," Freeman said, "you might want to wait until you see what disciplinary action is taken by the police department. In a strange way, it may be more beneficial for you to be relieved of your duty and be awarded your pension and benefits. In the face of any such eventuality, you could then be drawing a healthy salary based on your years on the force, and this income would be gravy."

"Gravy?" Earl said with a grin. "This job would be charity! You don't think I'd *pay* him, do you?"

"You couldn't afford me," Wally said, continuing to pace. "This is something I'm gonna hafta talk over with the old lady—my wife. My former wife, I mean."

"You've got the years," Freeman said. "My advice would be to file for an immediate leave of absence. Until they confirm any wrongdoing and press official charges, they can't tell you what to do with your time or tell you where you can or cannot be employed. Then you can run Mr. Haymeyer's agency here from the time he leaves for Springfield until such time as either of you decides to make it more permanent."

"And I could begin immediately to learn the ropes."

"There's enough to do on the Bemis case alone," Earl said. "You can learn the ropes by osmosis, or from your first two employees. I had hoped to have this Bemis thing completed by the time I leave, but the pressure wouldn't be so intense now if I knew you'd be stepping in."

"But Earl, I'm not a manager. I've proved that over the years."

"Baloney. Bonnie'll run the business for you, and Philip and Margo here are so enamored of you they'll do anything you say. How 'bout it, you old coot?"

"You don't really expect an answer right away, do you?"

"I can wait a minute or two."

"Nah. I'll think about it, Earl. That's all I can say. No promises. I've put in a lotta years where I am right now. I hate to get run out by a jerk. I'll miss the place."

"But you'll be your own boss."

"Yeah," Wally said slowly, breaking into a huge, toothy grin. "I know."

The possibility was too good to be true. I caught Margo's eye. She was thinking the same thing.

"One thing I gotta get straight right now, Freeman," Wally said.

Lieutenant Freeman was startled. "Sir?"

"Will you represent me?"

"Before the police department, sir? Absolutely. I thought you'd never ask."

"And also in my personal financial dealings? I'm gonna need help in getting set up for self-employment and all. And I'll need someone to negotiate with the owner of this agency if I'm really gonna pursue this."

"That negotiation won't take long," Earl joked.

"Well, I'm not sayin' I'm gonna do it, but if I do, I wanna be represented, just like these millionaire free agents. That's what I'm gonna be. I'm gonna play out my option and become a free agent. I want a multi-year, no-cut contract, Haymeyer."

"I'll discuss it with your agent," Earl said.

Wally glanced around at each of us, trying to hide his

excitement and trying to gauge what we were thinking. "Can I do one thing, Earl? Just for the fun of it?"

"Name it."

"Can I sit in your chair, behind your desk, just to get a feel for it?"

"Before I'm through with it? I've gotta use that chair another three weeks. Forget it!"

"Lindsey Bemis is on line two for you, Earl," Bonnie said. "And by the way, I can handle this guy if he thinks he can handle this shop." She winked at Wally, who blushed.

After Earl took the phone he asked Lindsey if she minded if he put her on the box so everyone in the room could hear the conversation.

"First of all, I saw the paper," she said. "I didn't tell Timothy about it when I saw him today, because I didn't want to dash his hopes."

Earl told her why she needn't worry about EH giving up the case or even about Wally's having to drop out of the investigation which she was relieved to hear. "For some reason, Timothy finally believes I'm on to something that might help him. He's starting to work out in his cell and has gained a lot of weight and strength. He's off dope, and I can see a lot of life in his eyes. He told me the reason he had so little fight in him last time was that he was still able to get dope and it was ruining his will.

"He said prison in this country is like freedom compared to the rat holes he was in in Asia, so he was content to just enjoy it for a while. Now that he's in maximum security, the dope is there if he wants it badly enough, but he was able to kick the habit and he's doing his best to stay away from the sources. It's not easy because the sources need the users, you know.

"Anyway, I thought you'd want to know that Timothy might be at a point where he can actually help defend himself this time. He's been wracking his brain for memories that might prove he had been in the country only a few days when the murder took place. Even though he can be placed within a few miles of the scene, he feels the key will be establishing that the same person who committed the crimes in Texas and Arizona and New Mexico is the one who committed the murder. Then if he can somehow prove that he's never been in the Southwest, he's innocent in Chicago."

"Not bad thinking for a man in his condition," Earl said. "It's the same hypothesis Wally came up with a few days ago."

"Hey, hi, Lindsey!" Wally said.

"Hi, Sergeant!"

"Listen, if they bust me for helpin' you, maybe I'll see if I can't get sent to a federal pen and Tim and I can sit in the same cell and figure this thing out together!"

"Not funny," she said, laughing anyway.

"Did Earl tell you that your friend Freeman here is gonna represent me too?"

"No! Is that right? Is he there? Hi, Harold!"

"Hi, Lindsey!" Freeman appeared ill at ease.

"Are we still on for tomorrow night, Harold?" came the reason he was ill at ease.

"Yeah, right," he said, suddenly less articulate than he had been all day.

"Good! I'm looking forward to it!"

"Yeah, me too," he said, wanting to end the conversation. Wally was really giving him the eye and grinning. We were all enjoying it, especially Bonnie.

"Listen, Lindsey," Earl said, "when can we see Timothy, how many can come, and all that?"

"There's another visitation day in two weeks, but Harold was telling me at dinner last night that his counsel can see him almost any time and that there is flexibility in the number of visitors. I should think Harold could arrange that, couldn't you, Harold?"

"Yes, yes, I probably could." Poor Harold had no more secrets.

"I'll be assigning Wally to head up this case if he has the time, so I'll leave it to him regarding who should visit Timothy first. Meanwhile, is there anything else we need to know?"

"Just that I'm grateful and that I'm looking forward to working with you all on this."

"Some of us more than others, huh Lindsey?" Wally needled.

"Oh, Wally!"

Freeman headed back to the Great Lakes Naval Training Station, and the rest of us killed the rest of the afternoon brainstorming the case. "I think the kid's on to something when he says we need to prove the murder was committed by the same person who pulled the jobs in the Southwest," Wally said. "We've gotta establish that and then come up with a solid alibi for Bemis during those years. If he really was still in 'Nam all that time, it should be easy to prove. I mean, we're not gonna have the other Bemis, whoever he is, dropped in our lap."

"The thing I don't get," Margo said, "is how the Chicago murder could be so coincidental with Timothy's return from overseas. Is it likely that whoever was using his identity knew he had arrived and set him up? And if so, why? Just to finally lay to rest the suspicion for the crimes in the Southwest? And also, is it possible Bemis could have stowed away all the way from 'Nam to the East Coast with no one on that ship seeing him or remembering him?"

"I'm encouraged that he's working on his memory of those things," Earl said. "It appears to me that he didn't give Freeman too much to go on the first time around. Maybe it's too much to ask, but I'd like to think he could dredge up something now—now that his mind and body are coming back to life—that would open the door on this crazy thing."

"What I want," Wally said, "is a reunion between someone who saw him on that ship, or a reunion of my fist with the face of the guy who used Bemis's identity for so long. You know, of course, Earl, that when we find that guy, he's gonna have been one of Uncle Sam's finest."

" 'Fraid so, Wally. Speaking of what we want, you know what I want?"

"Prob'ly."

"I want you at EH."

"I was right."

NINE

Wally Festschrift's showing up with his own counsel at the police department hearing caused a furor in the press like Chicago hadn't seen for years. Freeman sought and received a continuance, an unconditional leave of absence for his client for whatever amount of time it took to decide his fate, and assurances that Wally would receive full benefits and pension and any compensatory time due him if he was cleared.

Most significant, according to reporters, was Freeman's "threat" that there was always the possibility of countersuit for defamation of character, libel, slander, and violation of personal freedoms protected under the U.S. Constitution.

"The police review board," chirped the *Tribune*, "may pretend it was unimpressed with what it calls Sergeant Festschrift's overreaction to the inquiry, but they cannot deny that they are now tangling with an impressive young barrister in Harold Freeman, only recently honorably discharged from the U.S. Navy."

With Wally free to be gainfully employed wherever he wished, he was assigned to Larry Shipman's old desk until May 16 when he would be allowed to move into Earl's office.

Both Earl and Wally made it clear to Margo and Bonnie and me that this didn't necessarily mean that Wally would be taking over the agency. "The most important thing now," lawyer Freeman kept reminding us, "is to get Sergeant Festschrift fully cleared and free to rejoin the police force with no encumbrances or limitations. Then he would be able to choose to resign with full benefits *and* enjoy his new career." That always resulted in a grin from Wally.

The first morning he spent in the office, Wednesday, May 4, Wally couldn't sit still. He kept pacing, getting used to the filing system, asking Bonnie and Earl and everyone else all kinds of questions, rubbing his hands together and saying, "I hate office work, but this is fun, huh? Huh?"

We'd nod and smile and watch the clutter build on his desk as he finally got into gear and started feverishly piecing together the elements he hoped would free Timothy Bemis. "We gotta talk to that guy as soon as possible," he said, grabbing the phone and trying to dial out without knowing the phone system idiosyncracies.

"May I assume you're trying to reach Mr. Freeman, Walvoord?" Bonnie asked in her most formal and official tone.

"Yeah, what do I do?"

"One moment, please. I'll buzz you when he's on the line."

"OK, great. His number is ah, ..."

"I have his number, thank you, Walvoord," she said, dialing. In seconds, Wally's phone buzzed. He thought the buzz meant that he should pick up the receiver. Bonnie shouldn't have been able to hear him other than on the intercom, but he bellowed loud enough to be heard down the block.

"Yeah, whadya got?"

"What I've got, Mr. Festschrift, is Mr. Freeman on your line."

"Oh! Thanks!" he said.

"You don't have to pick up the receiver to talk to me on the intercom."

"Huh? I don't? Sorry," he said, slamming the receiver down again.

"Well, now you've just hung up on your party," Bonnie informed him.

"Well, for cryin' out loud! You shoulda just showed me how to dial him myself!"

"I'll be happy to do that when we have enough time, Mr. Festschrift, but we close in five hours."

"Oh, you're cute. Call 'im again, will ya?"

Bonnie answered the phone. "No need, it's him. I'm transferring him to you." And Wally's phone rang.

"Now can I answer this, or will I set off a shower of sparks over here?"

"Yes, you may answer it," she said, amused in spite of herself.

"Yeah, Freeman? Hey, you're a hard guy to get ahold of. . . . You been there all morning? Well, me too, you know what I mean? I gotta get outa this place. . . . Listen, I got all my ducks in a row, and it's time some of us talked to Bemis. What can you arrange? . . . I don't know, hang on. Hey, everybody, how many of us need to talk to Bemis?"

"I'd like to," Margo said, "but you know I'm off next week and the week after the wedding, so I don't suppose I'd do much good, especially if you have to limit his visitors."

Earl called out from his office: "Wally, why don't you just take Philip and Freeman with you? We don't all need to go. You can fill us in later."

It shocked me to realize that Margo had just two more working days with the agency in its present form. What would we come back to after our honeymoon? Would Wally and Bonnie have meshed professionally by then? It was apparent he was going to have to establish early who was boss, if indeed he was going to be.

For sure, it was going to be a different place without Earl. Earl had come to the point where he let us do most of the legwork. He was in on anything dangerous or important, but whatever we could handle, he let us. Wally would want to be in on everything. That was OK with me. In many ways he would be a lot like Earl when we were out of the office. I'd never met two guys who knew more people, more angles, more tricks. It was in the office that would prove the biggest difference in personalities.

Earl ran a tight ship, a clean, organized place. That responsibility would fall to us now; in fact, we'd likely be picking up after Wally if we wanted his office clean. We weren't worried about it. Wally was Wally. He'd be worth the work.

I was glad Margo had arranged to take off the week before the wedding. There was so much she wanted to do. Her father would be flying in from Chicago to give her away. My parents would drive over from Dayton to see Chicago and meet Margo for the first time. Friends from church, as well as everyone from the office, would have a part in the wedding. We were really looking forward to it.

When Wally got off the phone he asked me to take a walk with him. We just went a few blocks, but it seemed to revive him. "Not much of an office person," he said, shaking his head. "Listen, it's just our luck. Bemis has been transported in from the federal penitentiary to the United States Veterans Hospital just southwest of the Great Lakes Naval Training Center for several days of physical and psychological testing. Freeman likes that because he can get his own shrink in there to verify that Bemis's memory is sound and all that.

"Anyway, we're set to see him tomorrow morning at about nine. What I'd like to do, if you don't mind—and even if you do, ha, that was a joke, kid, get it?—is to get up there real early in the morning. I don't know about you, but I'm a morning person myself. I'd like to just work in the car on the shores of Lake Michigan up there somewhere at about six or seven o'clock, poring over all our stuff and coming up with a schedule, a list of questions we need answers to, so when we see him, we'll be ready and we'll get what we need. Huh? Sound all right with you?"

"Just one question, Wally. Is one of us going to have to go

to the Southwest and dig into these crimes apparently committed by Bemis's double?"

"I don't know, but if we find out we should, it'll be you. I can't leave the state. I hafta be available for all this internal affairs baloney. You know, a guy who used to work in Homicide with Earl and me years ago is the chief in Phoenix now. I'll bet he would have access to the whole file on Bemis out there. What I'd like to know is whether this character lived as Bemis for years, or just pulled this ID out of the hat when he needed it. Of course Margo raised a good point last night, too, about whether this guy knew Bemis was back in the country or if that Chicago murder was just a lucky coincidence that got him off the hook. The thing is, whoever that guy was, he's not using Bemis's identity anymore, at least not if and when he gets busted. He knows a good thing when he sees one. If he's smart, and being a doper he probably isn't, he'll go into hiding for a few years and then go straight. The Bemis identity has kept him on the streets for a long time."

"Well, I just want you to know, Wally, that I'm willing and ready to go to the Southwest if you need me. The only thing I have to be back for is my wedding, and I suppose Margo would appreciate it if I were back a day or two ahead of that."

"Yeah, I imagine she would. We'll have you back in time, kid. Fact is, I wanna have this thing wrapped up before Earl leaves, and that means before your wedding, too."

"I *would* need some coaching on what to look for out in Phoenix, if I go," I said.

"Hey, if Lew McCormick is still chief in Phoenix, you won't need to know diddly. He'll give you everything they've got. Cops like Lew live and die for justice, which is more than I can say for my prima donna 'colleague' downtown. But we're not gonna talk about him, are we?"

"I'm not."

"Me either. The creep."

That night at dinner, Margo filled me in on all the wedding plans. "And has Earl agreed to be best man yet?" she asked.

"No, but he's agreed to be there. I told him he was going to be an usher, so he's renting a tux, but I want to surprise him with the best-man business."

"How long are you going to wait before you tell him?"

"I don't know. I thought maybe I'd wait until he had ushered for a while; that way I could get double duty out of him!"

Margo shook her head. "Incurable but, luckily, not contagious."

Margo had put Bonnie in charge of arrangements with the florist and caterer, and she would be in charge of making sure the women in the bridal party got to the sanctuary in one piece. "She's just eating this up, Philip. And her granddaughter, Erin, will be in the wedding."

"And what about you?"

"Oh, hadn't you heard? I'm going to be the bride."

"Now who's incurable? I mean, what are you thinking about all this by now? Scared? Still excited?"

"Both. More than ever. You getting cold feet?"

"Nah. It's scary sometimes though, when I think about it. But I like to think about it."

"Me too," she said, taking my hand. "Actually, I'm really getting into it. I waited a lot of years for the right man."

"I thought you said there weren't any others."

"There weren't. That's why I waited. You are worth the wait."

"I'd like to think you mean that."

"You know I do, Philip. I'm giving up a life of ease for you."

"You tried. I wouldn't take it, remember?"

"And you don't want me to keep it either, remember?"

"So what are you going to do with it?" I asked.

"From the way you asked that, I'm guessing you'd be surprised to think that I already have a plan."

"You're right. It's not like you haven't had enough other things to think about."

"Well, I do have a plan, and you're going to like it."

"Oh, I am, huh? You know me pretty well, don't you?"

"Better than you think."

"That's probably true."

"I'm just teasing, Philip, but I do know you well enough to know that this is going to strike a chord with you. This is a Spencian idea if I've ever had one. When I prayed about this, as I said I was going to, I got to thinking about how tough a time I had in accepting Mothers death.

"Remember, I was a new Christian, and I was counting heavily on the promise that God would give me the desires of my heart if I put my trust in Him. The desire of my heart was that my mother become a Christian, and the next thing I knew, she was dead.

"I know you felt inadequate trying to explain the mind and workings of God, and as I recall, you pretty much admitted that sometimes all we can do is trust Him, know that His ways are better than our ways and that His thoughts are better than ours, and believe that, because He sees the big picture, He knows best."

"Yeah, and I think I put you onto Job where Job finally comes to the conclusion that man is in no position to question God even when nothing seems to make sense."

"The best thing you gave me, I think, was that apparently the interpretation of the phrase 'give you the desires of your heart' might be better understood if it said 'will tell you what the desires of your heart should be.' Either that or the way it reads in Scripture puts a lot more emphasis on the prerequisites than most Christians can live up to. Otherwise we'd all get everything we want, even though God knows better than to give us everything we think we want.

"Now that you're wondering what all this is leading to, here it is: God has given me the desire of my heart."

"You mean he gave you something you wanted?"

"No, Philip, he gave me a *desire*. He gave me the desire to see many, many people come to Him. When I was going through all that trauma with Mother, the desire of my heart was that she come to Christ. That was God-honoring and it was a worthy desire, but it wasn't necessarily a desire God had given me. God thinks bigger than we do. So the desire He has given me is bigger than that.

"My desire is that *everyone* should come to Christ, that, as the Bible says, none should perish but all should come to repentance. I know the desire is one God has given me because it's straight from Scripture. What's interesting about it is that it's actually less realistic than the original desire I had. Isn't it more realistic to desire one person's salvation than that of the whole world? Yet that is the will of God according to the Bible.

"My desire for my mother, though honorable, was selfish. It was for me, not for the glory of God, even though her salvation would have glorified Him. I have to tell you, I still don't like it much that it didn't happen, and I can still cry myself to sleep remembering that she died without God. But God has given me His desire, His will, and, ironically through Mother's death, He has also provided a way in which I can contribute to it and see it somewhat fulfilled.

"A main scriptural principle is that life comes from death. If you want to find your life, lose it. If you want to lead, serve. If you want to live, die. The death of winter results in the life of spring. Mother's death was not in vain. From her death can come life eternal for many people if I put that money in the hands of the right people.

"So, what I have taken so long to say is that I have been studying ministries that need money. To read their literature, you would think they all do, and maybe they do. But very soon I'm going to find one or two that are on the front lines, using their time and energy to win people to Christ. And when I feel led to give the money where it will be used most effectively for spreading the Gospel, that's where it will go as anonymous gifts."

She sat with her elbows on the table, a fist on each cheek, staring at me in the dimly lit restaurant. I was speechless. What had happened to this woman? I had seen her grow, sure. She was an entirely different person from the one I had met not so long ago. But what was this? This was wisdom. This was maturity. The sad fact, what this made clear, was that she was breezing past me, her erstwhile spiritual counselor, at ninety miles an hour.

"So, what do you think, Philip? Am I going off half-cocked, or what? It feels right, but I've learned that feelings are not always a good barometer. I want to do what God wants me to do, and that means what I do has to be consistent with the Bible, right?"

I nodded. "Those Sunday school classes and neighborhood Bible studies have really made an impact on you, haven't they?"

"That and the good preaching we've heard—just straight Bible. I like that."

"Me too. But, Margo, I don't now what to say. I'd better marry you quick, or I'll be losing you to the mission field or some seminary somewhere."

"So it sounds all right to you?"

"It sounds better than all right, Margo. It sounds like I'd better get serious about my own Bible study before I get lost in the dust."

"That's not a good enough reason, though, is it?"

"Not a good enough one, no. But see? It's happened already. You're so tuned in that you can even see through my pseudo-spiritual motives. I'm going to love being married to you."

"Don't be too sure; it's not all as selfless as it appears."

"How do you mean?"

"The toughest part was deciding on the anonymous approach. Ooh, I hate to admit that."

I laughed. "How refreshing to know that you're still human! Uh, I suppose I should still pay for dinner, huh, Moneybags?"

"You're terrible."

The next morning, Wally and I got a 5:30 start for the veterans' hospital south of Great Lakes Naval Training Center. I must have looked pretty mopey.

"Not a morning person, huh, kid?"

"Oh, yeah, usually. It's just that the night before last I didn't sleep much because I was upset with Margo. And last night I had trouble falling asleep because I was so thrilled with her."

Wally didn't respond. He just shook his head and handed me a thick sheaf of folders. "That's what we're gonna be discussing at the beach," he said. "We wanna be ready for the most important interview we'll have in this case."

TEN

Wally parked as near the water as he could, and the rising sun was magnified off the windshield and warmed the car to the perfect temperature for going back to sleep. But you don't sleep when Walvoord F. Festschrift is holding forth.

"So, what'd ya find in the files there, boy?"

"I found that Tim Bemis's memory better be pretty good because we need something or somebody that will corroborate his story that he was out of the country when the crimes in the Southwest were perpetrated."

"Wow, you sound just like a PRO-fessional law enforcement type. *Perpetrated?* Very impressive. Anyway, you're right, of course. But you wanna know what's been stickin' in my craw? I thought the prosecution was pretty weak during the trial—you can see it here in the court transcripts—when the defense implied they had not established a clear motive in the murder."

"Yeah. You mean when Freeman pushed them on it and they came up with that criminal psychologist who talked about Bemis's having freaked out when he saw the postal uniform, identifying it with his military days and all that."

"Of course it was rubbish," Wally said, "and as Freeman accurately pointed out at that time, that kind of reasoning only points to another killer. If Bemis had been in this country long enough to commit the earlier crimes, why hadn't any of them been against people in uniform? And if Bemis was the type who would freak out at the sight of a uniform, why hadn't he accosted any of the conductors on the train from Norfolk to Chicago? Anyway, what kind of whacko would plan a murder like that? Senseless as it was, it had to be planned. The guy had to strap that mine to his belt, get in line, wait his turn, and do his thing. You gotta think that victim was a target, that there had to have been a motive."

Wally doubled his fists and tapped on the steering wheel and the dashboard, thinking. "We've gotta get more on the murder victim. The guy was supposed to have been a drifter with a history of civil service work. He had been divorced for several years, no known children. Only a few co-workers and neighbors came to the funeral. I mean, this was about as anonymous a kind of a guy as you could find. The real victory by the prosecution, in my book, was that they somehow evoked some sympathy for the victim out of that jury."

"So, what makes you think he was a specific target of the murderer?"

"The biggest reason is I don't think whoever did this did it to frame Bemis. I'm convinced his double is somebody who was in the service with him, got to know everything about him, and then used his identity when he was sure Bemis wasn't coming back. Probably a doper; well, we know that from the criminal record which all went against Bemis's name, of course.

"And you know the judge wouldn't allow the prosecution to admit evidence from the Arizona criminal file on Bemis because he said it would have no bearing on this case. That worked against Bemis, because if there *was* a fingerprint file on him, it would have proved conclusively if he had ever been in that state before. I can't figure his double, though.

"Murder wasn't his style. He had kept to himself, to his home area. All these crimes were confined to those three states. Then he ups and heads for Chicago, goes to one place, murders one man, for one reason. What was the reason? Give me the reason, and I'll give you your man. What we've got to do is to match the guy who was using Bemis's name in the Southwest with the murder victim. And then we have to trace the murderer to Southeast Asia through military records to the time Bemis was over there."

"But would it have been a buddy of his, Wally? Someone in his company?"

"No. In fact, it almost had to be an Army guy because those types of mines are exclusive to the Army."

"Then it was someone in a prison camp with Bemis."

"Likely."

"Someone who might have told everything to Bemis about his own background and vice versa?"

"Sure, Philip. Guys who think they're never coming back do that sort of thing. The guy who would never have the guts to ask you how you got a scar on your forehead—and who you would never volunteer the information to in a million years—could get your whole life story out of you in a few days in a prison camp."

On the way to the hospital, Wally stopped off to call the office and ask Margo to invest some time on the phone and to pore over the records to see what we could find about the deceased Lloyd Cavenaugh that neither lawyer had thought to look for before.

We met Freeman in the lobby. He was excited—still formal and overly articulate, but excited. "He looks super, Sergeant Festschrift, he really does. The difference between now and the last time I saw him, well, I wouldn't have believed it if I hadn't seen it myself. The man must have gained fifty pounds, and all muscle."

"More like about thirty-eight," Timothy Bemis told us as we sat across the table from him in the maximum security wing of the medical facility. "I got the idea from some of the guys in the slam. They beat the boredom by working out, and I mean working out all day and half the night. I'm not kidding you, I know a guy who works out about twelve hours a day. The doc made them give him vitamins and let him eat more because he was tearing himself down at first. He's gained about eighty pounds of muscle. Push-ups, chin-ups, sit-ups, weights, you name it, he does it all. Even when he's alone in his cell, we can hear him grunting through hour after hour of workouts. I think he wants to be a boxer or something."

"Let me just comment on something, if I may, Timothy, before I let these gentlemen ask you some questions," Freeman said. "What you just said is the longest single piece of conversation I have ever heard from you. Are you aware of that?"

"No. Well, yeah, I guess."

"I wanted to pity you the last time we worked together, but frankly, it was infuriating. It took me a long time to realize that it was the result of malnutrition, psychological damage from the prison camps and your subsequent ordeals, and the effect of the drugs that made it impossible for you to respond. Do you recall how you reacted to me?"

"Sort of," Bemis said with a weak smile. "It was like, um, like you woke me up to talk to me each time and all I wanted to do was go back to sleep. I knew you were trying to help me, and I knew you were trying to help Lindsey, but I couldn't think. I couldn't talk. I couldn't do anything. The thing I'm afraid of now is that I won't be able to remember things that happened when I was so out of it."

"Well," Freeman said, "we're going to just have to work through that and take a positive approach. We're going to assume your memory has returned with your body and your psyche. All right? I'm assuming you care about clearing yourself; that's the most important thing."

"Yeah, that has become very important to me. For a strange reason too, I think. It's mostly because Lindsey is giving her life to this goal of gettin' me out. For a long time I was so wasted that I honestly didn't know whether I snuffed the guy or not. I really didn't. But, hey, if there's anything I'm sure of now, it's that I didn't do those things down there in Texas. I've never been there in my life. I also know I had just got back to this country a few days before I got to Great Lakes, and I never left that train."

"OK. All right," Wally said. "May I?"

Freeman nodded.

"Now, Timothy," Wally began, "I'm going to assume that even though you're doing great with your weight and your responses and all—and your new teeth look great, by the way—you're probably not used to extended conversation, grilling, interrogation, that type of thing. So what I want to do is start with the toughest stuff early.

"Let me tell you this: the first thing we're going to do in this investigation is the easy part, and that is proving once and for all that there are two Timothy Bemises, and one is an impostor. With our contacts in Phoenix, we can match fingerprints in their file and establish that. Then if we're lucky enough to find out that the other Bemis pulled a job when we know beyond a shadow of a doubt you were on your way to Great Lakes, then we're getting somewhere.

"But for the questioning, I want you to wrack your brain while it's fresh."

"I'm not too sure that it's, ah, fresh, 'cause they've been puttin' me through a lot of stuff here already."

"Well, all right, we'll just do the best we can. The first thing is, we need to know who your friends were in 'Nam. Who would have known enough about you, would have looked enough like you, and would have had knowledge of the type of land mine used to murder Lloyd Cavenaugh?"

Bemis buried his head in his hands and groaned. "Oh, man, there were so many Army guys, you know? And it's been so long. When we got onto the mainland there, it seemed like everyone we had any contact with was regular Army."

"But would they have known everything about you? Your tag numbers? Your Social Security number, all that?"

"No, no way."

"Would they have asked about your scar in case they wanted to duplicate it someday?"

"Every once in a while someone would ask me. I was very private about it, though. I didn't tell anyone until I got into the camps. Then you didn't care who you told what. We used to sit there and recite everything we could remember about each other, and I mean *everything*. We'd memorize everyone's statistics in case we ever got out and could tell their families or mail some notes or whatever."

Festschrift leaned forward in his chair. "Timothy, this is the key. Someone in one of those camps took that information. Everything, down to the exact way you got your scar, your mother's maiden name, your statistics, your *numbers*. Man! I want you to get mad about this person, Tim. I want you to get excited about him. I want you to realize that he's a murderer and he put you here. Someone you probably would have helped if you'd escaped, if what your sister said about you is true. Wrack your brain, Bemis, tell me about those guys. Who were they?"

Tim just looked at Festschrift as if he wasn't catching his drift. Wally had had the desired effect on Freeman and me. We were excited; we were hot about the injustice of it all. Wally knew how to put things in perspective. When Bemis didn't answer, Wally kept trying.

"This guy, whoever he was, is the one who's been wasting your sister's life."

"Mr., um, uh, Fester—"

"Call me Wally."

"Mr. Wally, I don't think you realize how many different camps I was in—dozens, man—how long ago it's been and what has happened to me since then."

"But you said you guys sat around memorizing each other's numbers."

"But we were sick. We were starving. We were beaten. We'd get to know a guy by talking to him through the wall for thirty-six hours, then he'd be gone who knows where and you'd never hear of him again."

"This had to be someone who saw you, Bemis. This guy has injured himself precisely the way you did, probably with the same thing. Solder, right?"

"Right," Bemis said, suddenly sitting up and gazing in the distance. "You're right, this guy had to have seen me. There was only a couple or three camps where we could see each other." He talked slowly, reciting in a monotone now. "I was the only Navy guy in Da Nang. Every day at about noon they'd drag us out into a courtyard and chain us to metal poles, and we'd burn in the sun for hours, becoming delirious.

"The religious guys would sing hymns and say Bible verses and stuff and pray. I prayed, too. You get religious real quick over there. But we faced each other and we would talk. And my scar would burn bright red because there was no protection, and I had to tell everybody about the accident.

"You didn't care anymore. It was like if you didn't leave somebody, even somebody who had just as good a chance to die right there as you did, if you didn't leave them with your story, your background would die right there with you.

"For a while I remembered all those guys, but, but—" He bit his lip and his chin quivered. "But I couldn't, I couldn't—oh, please! I couldn't remember each day who was still alive. Sometimes I thought I was dead."

He sobbed.

"We can wait," Wally said.

"No! I want to tell this. I can feel sorry for anybody who was there, but somebody who would use a fella's private story, the story he told only hoping that when he died someone would survive and take part of him back to the States with him, that's bad. That person I don't feel sorry for."

"You've gotta remember something about these people, Timothy. A first name, a last name, a serial number, a hometown."

Bemis moaned. "They were from all over, and their stories all got jumbled together. I'd ask somebody something about what he'd said the day before, and he'd tell me it wasn't him, it was the guy who was buried that morning."

Wally stood and walked to the caged window. Peering out, he swore. "I can't expect you to remember anything specific. This is impossible. Are you up to another try on a different subject, something more recent?"

"Maybe. I'm sorry. I'll try."

"Hey, it's not your fault, Bemis. But I'll tell you this, you come up with one shred of information and we'll get our teeth into it like a bulldog on a milkman's pant leg."

Bemis tried to smile. "What else can I try to help you with?"

"The ship you stowed away on. A Navy vessel, you say."

"It had to be. I tried to board a couple of U.S.-bound cargo ships. One was bringing in textiles and carrying out rubber, but I didn't know enough about the ship to know where to go. When the Navy ship docked, I dressed like a Vietnamese and carried sailor's purchases aboard with other Vietnamese. I was so thin I could hide under the wide hat, and I was so sick that I could impersonate an elderly man easily.

"As soon as I got on board, I knew where to hide. I had enough food to last about two weeks, and I also knew where and when to steal food from the holds."

"Somebody had to have seen you during the trip back," Wally tried. "They just had to."

Bemis stood now too. "Yes," he said, "someone did."

Wally wheeled around. "Who?"

"I don't know, but I remember being found. I was so sick.

Man, I was desperate. I wanted to get back to Great Lakes so bad, and I didn't know who to trust. I didn't know what had happened in the war. I didn't know if I was still considered a deserter or AWOL or what. I didn't want to be thrown overboard or tortured or tried or anything."

"Timothy," Wally said gently, "you have got to piece this crisis episode together for me, slowly, so a description or a name or something comes back to you. We can find out what ship was in Vietnam waters around that time, and we can get a list of the men aboard, but give me something to go on."

Bemis sat again and held his hands to his head almost as if he were about to go to sleep. "I was stealing some potatoes from the hold one morning, after midnight. I was sick, too sick to move. I lay down on a sack of potatoes and the pain in my stomach, down here (he pointed to his abdomen), made me curl up in a ball like a baby. I tried not to let any noise come out, and I thought I was doing pretty well, but I must have fallen asleep.

"My own cry woke me up just as the door opened and a flashlight blinded me. I drew myself up tighter and whimpered, even though I was trying hard not to." Bemis was lost in his memory now, as if unaware we were even still there. He mimicked the voice of his captor. "'You got troubles, sailor?' He was a petty officer, second class."

"How in the world can you remember that it was a—"

Wally was interrupted by a gesture from Freeman, and he let Bemis continue. He was crying again. "I was so close to freedom. I thought about killing him! But I knew I didn't have the strength. I was more afraid I would die right there. I reached up with all the strength I had left and grabbed him by the lapels with both hands. I squeezed so hard I broke the skin on one hand. I pulled him almost in on top of me, and when he resisted I squeezed harder and wrenched his head down close to mine. He pulled back when I opened my mouth because the flashlight was between us now and he could see my face and my infected gums, and my trench mouth must have just about gagged him.

"I said, 'Don't call for help. Whatever you do, don't call for help.' And you know what he said? You know what he called me? He called me an old man. He said, 'I don't know how you got here, old man, but I've got to get you some help.'

"And I said, 'Please, oh please, oh please. If you never do anything for anyone else as long as you live, Keller, just let me stay here and don't tell anyone I'm here.' I was so desperate and so ugly and so pitiful that I knew he would do what I asked. I didn't let go of his coat for the longest time. My hands were frozen solid in the grip. He peeled me away and said OK, and I believed him.

"He said, 'You can't ever tell anybody about this either, then, old timer.' And I cried, thanking him and promising him."

Bemis's head was on the table, and he sobbed. Wally leaned down and put his arm around him. "Tim, just tell me. Why did you call him Keller?"

Bemis lifted his head slowly, displaying bloodshot eyes. His voice was thick, as if he had just awakened. "Huh?" he said.

"You called him Keller, buddy. Why did you call him Keller?"

He stared at the wall again. "I could see his name tag. It said Keller. But you can't get him in trouble."

Wally smiled sympathetically. "He won't get into any trouble, Timothy. Will he, Freeman?"

"No, sir," Harold said. "Not if his intent was justice."

That sounded familiar.

ELEVEN

Wally left Harold Freeman with instructions to try to pinpoint the camps Bemis could remember being in before he lost his teeth and only those camps where the prisoners could see each other.

He then called Earl and got the three people back at the office working on the bureaucracy in Washington, trying to get a list of the big ships in Vietnam waters in April and May of 1981, something similar to the ship Bemis described which would have docked in Norfolk in early June.

Before we left for the office, Wally called a friend in Washington and asked about the possibility of getting a list of U.S. prisoners of war, categorized by which camps they were reported to have been in during the war.

He was told it could be done but it would take a few days, and he should try to narrow the request to as few camps as possible.

Then he called Lew McCormick in Phoenix. "You remember the Bemis case, Lew?" he asked his old friend. "Yeah, I know you *think* he was out there before he got busted back here, but what would you say if I told you I think your Bemis and our Bemis are two different guys? . . . Yeah, I'm serious. But listen, Lew, I'm not doin' this for the Chicago PD. This is strictly on my own, OK? Anything wrong with wirin' me his file? . . . Well, how 'bout just the prints then? . . . No prints? How in the world can you collar a guy on federal dope felonies and not pull prints? . . . I'm tellin' ya, Lew, my guy has never been west of the Mississippi. He's a blue-collar guy right outa the neighborhoods here. He's a wrong-way guy, yeah, but he's more'n paid for it. Listen, I at least need to know when he pulled his last job out there, anything during the spring of 1981. Send me what ya can, pal, and I'll 'preciate it. . . . Yeah, you too. Hi to Ethel. . . . No, you're kiddin'. I'm sorry, I didn't know. Me too, you know? . . . Yeah, coupla years back. We're seein' each other again a little though, so who knows? . . . Yeah, OK, Lew. Hang tough, buddy."

Wally slammed the phone down and swore. "Lew doesn't think they pulled one print on all those busts, can you believe it? Apparently the guy had a good lawyer, and he kept pushing the bit about having been a POW, so they spared him the indignity. They spared him the indignity right into a murder rap for someone else. Prints sure woulda made things easier, Philip."

"That means we have to find this Keller, huh?"

"You got it. If we can place Bemis on a ship during the month of May while he was supposed to be pullin' a job in the Southwest somewhere, we can at least prove there's two of 'em, prints or no prints."

Back at the office we got the word that the USS *California,* a nuclear-powered guided missile frigate carrying more than 550 men, left Vietnam in May 1981, for a two-week charge back to the United States, arriving Norfolk, June 2.

"That's our rowboat," Wally said, "and it was going for some sort of record, coming the long way around, rather than taking the Pacific route to San Francisco or San Diego. Now let's find the Keller who was a petty officer second class."

"I already tried," Margo said. "No such animal. There was a Keener, a Kellogg, and two Kendalls, all seaman apprentices or seamen. According to Earl's friend, none of them would have been issued a flashlight or been wearing petty officer insignias."

"Margo," Wally said wearily, "you gotta go back to that source. I wanna know the names of the petty officers on that ship."

"OK, Wally," she said. "Do you want to see what I got on Cavenaugh?"

"No, this takes priority. Ah, well, yeah. What'd ya get? Anything?"

"Well, I'm not sure. I got a complete resumé on him that wasn't entered into the court record. He had been a clerk in Chicago post offices since the late sixties, had a little attendance problem here and there, mostly due to drinking. The interesting thing is, in the court transcript they didn't go back beyond Chicago because he'd been there more than a decade, at three or four different branch offices. But look at this."

She slid the file right side up so Wally could read it. "Apparently he was a drifter for almost a year before coming to Chicago," she said, "but look what he did in 1971, after he'd been in Chicago two or three years. He filed for back seniority, based on previous civil service tenure with the postal service. It seems he had put in several years of service in Amarillo, Texas, from the time he returned from the Korean War until he quit in the late sixties and drifted to Chicago before starting over. It looked bad for him at first because the postal service maintained that he had quit and knew he would lose his seniority and civil service tenure unless it was a layoff. But he won the battle because of the testimony of his former boss in Amarillo who said Cavenaugh had quit under extenuating circumstances. Who knows what that meant? It was enough for the postal service, though."

"He didn't have a bad record at all in Texas," Wally said, scowling at the file. "Worked his way up from sorter and then carrier to clerk and even assistant postmaster. Not bad at all.

But there's no clue to the breakdown here. Why would he have thrown it over and got on the bottle? His divorce was back in the early fifties, and he had no kids. He had worked for the same boss for years, in fact, would likely have replaced him as postmaster within six or eight years when the guy retired, so I doubt there was a feud there. Hey, Earl? You mind if I keep Margo on this?"

"You're in charge of this case, Wally, and she's only here today and tomorrow. So do what you want."

"OK, Margo. Try to get hold of his former boss, the retired postmaster in Amarillo. Even if he's moved away, they oughta have *his* address, wouldn't you think? I'm putting Philip on this Keller thing."

"Phone for you, Wally," Bonnie said. "It's Mr. Freeman."

"Yeah, Freeman. . . . OK, good. Let me get that down. That'll help. By the way, no Keller on board that ship. . . . Nah, I don't know. We're still checking to see if it was something else. Listen, is there any reason a Navy guy's nameplate would have his first name instead of his last? No? Any other variations that would make sense? . . . Well, thanks."

While Margo was on the phone to Texas trying to locate the former postmaster, I was put on hold by Navy Information Services. I had used Earl's name to get to the right person, and she was trying to come up with a list of the petty officers on the *California*. There were several, and as I jotted them down, Wally towered over me and watched.

When I got to the L's and wrote Ladd, Lahr, Laughman, and Lauth, Wally reached over my shoulder and circled Lahr. "Ask her if there was another Lahr of any rank on that ship," he whispered.

"Excuse me, ma'am," I said, "I'm sorry to interrupt, but could you tell me if there was another Lahr on board?"

"Just one, sir, as a petty officer."

"Any others at other ranks?"

"One moment please," she said, annoyed. "Yes, sir, I show a William Lahr as a seaman."

"And could you give me a first name of the petty officer Lahr."

"That would be Kenneth, sir."

When I wrote that down, Wally told me to tell her that was all we needed, except where to locate Kenneth Lahr. While she was looking that up, Wally said, "Freeman says if there's a common last name on board ship or on a base or anywhere, the men might use their first initial before their name on the tag. To a starving stowaway, K. Lahr could look like Keller, couldn't it?"

I nodded and took the information. Kenneth Lahr was now a chief petty officer in charge of training in San Diego. It took me until the next morning to get him on the phone.

Meanwhile, Margo had traced the former postmaster of Amarillo, Texas, to St. Petersburg, Florida, where his wife told her that he had died about six months before. Margo asked if by any chance she remembered Lloyd Cavenaugh.

"Oh, yes," the woman said sadly in a heavy Texas accent. "We were so fond of Lloyd. And shocked when he was murdered so senselessly. My husband always thought it so ironic that he was killed by a serviceman, him bein' a veteran himself. You know it was his duty on the draft board in Amarillo that finally drove him out of town. He'd been pretty tough on draft dodgers and even conscientious objectors, and when several of the boys he kept from avoidin' the draft either came back dead or wounded, or were listed missin', well, he seemed to have a change of heart and couldn't take it."

Wally whipped through his notes. "Freeman says Bemis narrowed down his prison camps, the ones where the other GIs could see him and where he still would have had his teeth, to Hanoi and Haiphong. We're going to want to match the list of Army regulars that Lloyd Cavenaugh had a hand in signing with the list Earl gets from Washington of all the

American prisoners who stayed in those camps during the years Bemis was there."

Friday morning's mail brought what there was of a file from Phoenix on the man authorities there thought was Timothy Bemis. All the statistics and numbers were Bemis's, but the photo—a glossy of the one Lindsey had shown us from the *Tribune,* looked less like Bemis than ever. The scar was there, but so were the teeth. It was the epitome of a drug-wasted young man—emaciated, blank-looking, drowsy. But we couldn't have gotten it to look like Tim Bemis if we'd been paid.

"Here's the best part," Wally said. "Somebody get on the horn and ask Lindsey to get in here. I think we can wrap this thing up today or tomorrow."

"Really?" Earl said, emerging from his office. We crowded around Wally.

"We need Kenneth Lahr's sworn testimony, which Philip should get this morning if we're lucky. That'll put Bemis on board the *California* during the last two weeks of May, right?" We all nodded. "Look at this bust in Tulsa, May 23. The man they think is Bemis knocked over an all-night drug-store. Unless our guy could have been two places at once, we've got an imposter."

"That doesn't mean our Bemis didn't murder Cavenaugh, Wally. You've still got to find the double and place him in Chicago at the time of the murder. Tim Bemis's train was at the station in Chicago long enough before continuing to Great Lakes that Bemis had the opportunity."

"But did he have the means, Earl? He could barely walk."

"The witnesses in the post office said the murderer limped badly. They also said he had the scar and was sickly and emaciated and looked desperate."

"But Bemis didn't know how to use that kind of weapon."

"He could have learned easily, having been in 'Nam. There wasn't much to the weapon, Wally."

"Earl, you sound like you don't think we're making any progress," Margo said.

"That's not it," Wally said. "Earl is the best devil's advocate in the business, and we need that right now to be sure we don't miss something or go off the deep end without everything covered. Earl, listen to this: our Bemis might have had the means—though that's doubtful—and he may have had the opportunity, though it would have been quite an ordeal for a guy in his condition. But even the jury the first time around had trouble with motive. Why Cavenaugh? What could Bemis have known about Cavenaugh?"

"I agree that's your key," Earl said. "Find out who the other Bemis is and establish a motive for him, and our man walks. It's as simple as that."

I called Kenneth Lahr at 11:00 Chicago time, 9:00 California time, and explained who I was and what I was after. "I represent a man who has been implicated in a crime committed May 23, 1981, in Tulsa, Oklahoma, when he claims he was aboard the USS *California*."

"Well, that should be easy to check, sir. We were sailing at that time, coming the long way around from Vietnam to Norfolk, Virginia. If the man was on board, it would be on our log."

"He was a stowaway, Mr. Lahr."

Silence.

"Tell me this, sir. He says you discovered him in the hold and that he begged you not to turn him in. Can you verify that? Sir? Mr. Lahr?"

Silence.

"Are you there, Mr. Lahr?"

"Well," he said, embarrassed, "I kind of have to be sure exactly who I'm talking to before I go talking about any untoward incidents aboard ship. You understand?"

"Yes. I can't prove to you who I am or who I am not, but I can try to assure you that nothing you tell me here can get you in trouble. All it can do is get an innocent man out of trouble."

"I see. Uh, I'm not saying I'm going to tell you unless I determine whether or not I need legal representation. I should stipulate right now that I may subsequently deny anything and everything I say."

"We may need you to testify in court on behalf of someone you could help exonerate. Would you at least agree to do that on the condition that we can keep you from legal retribution for any violation of military policies you may have committed?"

"For you, I will agree to that, and I can verify the action you described. But you must realize that this kind of infraction could cost me everything I've ever worked for."

"Sir, the man you kindly ignored that night is serving a life sentence for murder. You can help clear him and have our guarantee of free legal defense should you come up on charges for this, or you can rest in your comfortable rank."

There was a long silence. "Mr. Spence, you put in writing your offer of counsel and defense, which may prove unnecessary, you know, and I will do whatever is necessary. Fair enough?"

"Yes, sir. Fair enough."

Wally and Earl were ecstatic, and Margo agreed to work Saturday. We were expecting important mail. Through Earl's and Wally's contacts, we were getting lists of U.S. prisoners in Hanoi and Haiphong; and Margo had somehow finagled a list of draftees from Amarillo through friends of the former postmaster's wife. We would spend Saturday morning looking for matches and then trying the names out on Bemis, just in case.

It was unlikely he'd remember any by name, but it was worth the effort. We wanted someone who could pass for him. "With our luck," Wally said, "our only match will turn out to be a seven-foot black man."

That night, while Wally and Lindsey and Harold Freeman were visiting Tim Bemis, Margo and I had dinner with Earl and enjoyed talking about his new faith. And our wedding. "I want you to be best man," I said.

He looked stunned. "You're kidding. I thought I was supposed to be an usher."

"Wally and Larry Shipman are going to be ushers, along with a couple of guys from church. You'll all stand up with me, but I want you as best man."

"I'm flattered, Philip. I really am."

"And we're happy," Margo said. "You know, Earl, you've known us since before we were in love."

"Are you serious? If you weren't in love when I first met you, your faces were lying. I could tell. Tell me more about the wedding."

"Well, we've invited everyone from both churches, our current one and Philip's old church, I mean. The girls are making their own dresses. I'm buying mine. We're writing our own vows. The best part is my dad has insisted on paying for everything. That's the way it should be, I guess, but we haven't really been close for so long that it seems kind of strange."

"How many days now, Margo?"

"Eight. Nine including the day of the wedding. I need more time, Earl!"

"You say you're writing your own vows? Why is that?"

"Oh, we just want to be different, I guess. There's so much we want to say to each other publicly, and this will be the only chance we may ever get to do it. Our relationship has been a unique one, and there aren't any of the standard vows that really say it all. They're nice, and we'll incorporate some of them, but we want this to be really special. Not in a snooty way, just unique."

"Somehow, I think it'll be unique just because you two are in it," Earl said.

"Well, thank you, Earl," I said. He wasn't generally one to give an unconditional compliment.

"I hadn't really intended to include you in that remark, Philip," he came back with a grin. "It just sort of seemed like the right thing to do at the time. You know better than any of us that it's Margo who will make this wedding special."

I tried to look pained, but he had spoken the truth, as usual. "We want Christ to be glorified in it; that's the real point," I said.

Margo agreed.

"That'll make it unique all right," Earl said. "I don't think I've ever been to a wedding where Christ wasn't more than just part of the rhetoric. I'm looking forward to this one."

Me too, I thought, but saying it just sort of didn't seem like the right thing to do at the time.

TWELVE

Everybody was in the office the next morning, and I mean *everybody*. We arranged the desks in a big circle, and Earl passed out big stacks of computer printout sheets containing the names of all mid- and late-1960s draftees from the Texas Panhandle that would have been processed through the Amarillo draft board.

Armed with a smaller stack, Margo began reading through the names of GIs who had been imprisoned in the two camps Bemis had selected. For some reason, Margo's list was not alphabetized like the draftee list Earl had divvied up between us. It went by Social Security number, so all she could do was laboriously plow through it, reading aloud and giving the rest of us a chance to check the name against our lists.

Bonnie had *A* through *E*, Earl *F* through *I*. I had *J* through *N*, Harold Freeman had *O* through *S*, and Lindsey had *T* through *Z*. Wally just paced, shouting instructions, telling us what to look for, and instructing Margo how to go faster without making a mistake.

"Just read the last name, then the first name, then the Social Security number. If whoever has that letter in the alphabet determines that this particular Smith or Jones or whoever is not on his Texas list, he should sing out as soon as possible."

It was chaotic but almost fun. Margo would read a last

name. Without fail, there would be many servicemen by that last name on the alphabetized list. She would then read the first name and middle initial. The checker would say, "I've got that last name and three guys with that first name, two with that middle initial, none with that Social Security number."

"OK, all right," Wally would say. "We don't need a discourse. Just grunt or say something when you're sure you haven't got the guy and let her move on to the next name."

After about three hours of tedious checking and reading off hundreds of names, we started getting irritable. Bonnie let Wally take over her list, and she went out to get us something for lunch.

We had been rolling for only about five or six minutes with Wally in the saddle when we thought we'd gotten our first break. "Anderson with an *o*," Margo said. Wally rifled through his stacks.

"Pages and pages worth," he groaned. "Go ahead."

"Michael."

"Oh, that narrows it down to about a hundred names."

"Michael B."

"Uh-huh, I got a bunch."

She read off the number and Wally stood quickly, his chair rolling backward and crashing into the wall. "We've got a winner!" he said. "Wouldn't ya know we wouldn't get anywhere until ol' Festschrift gets in the game! Gimme the Social Security number again, just to be sure. Better yet, let me give you the one here and see if it matches yours. You oughta get some fun outa this too. Three-five-one, four-two, three-oh-one-oh."

"That's it!" Margo squealed.

"Released with last U.S. prisoners, April 1, 1973."

"Yes!"

"Agh!" And Wally swore. "Deceased August 2, 1975."

We all sat back and let out a collective sigh. "If you weren't on the outs with the Chicago PD, we could use their computer and cut this work by 90 percent," Earl teased.

"Jes' get back to work, Haymeyer," Wally said. "You ain't got many friends down there right now yerself."

It was in the early evening when we struck gold again. We'd eaten twice, grown sore and tired, and had taken to walking around carrying our stacks of paper with us. Freeman was spelling Margo on the reading, and she had taken his alphabetized lists. Bonnie was back at her own desk, and Wally was growing impatient.

"Harris," Freeman said.

"Uh-huh," Earl grunted. "Just a minute, there's lots of 'em."

"Raymond."

"Ah, there's not so many Raymonds."

"Raymond A."

"Got a couple, Harold. C'mon, tell me you've got a Raymond Albrecht Harris."

"You got it," Freeman said.

"Don't kid me, Harold."

"Harris, Raymond Albrecht, Social Security number three-four-seven, forty, four-two-three-six."

"That's the one," Earl said, trying to hide his enthusiasm. "Let me make sure this turkey's still living. Yup. Dishonorable discharge, overturned due to time spent in POW camp in Haiphong. Wally, call Billy at home. He'll know who to contact. We want to get this guy's numbers up on the screen tonight. Tell 'im we owe him one, huh?"

Earl dragged the papers back to Wally, who had to dial twice, he was so excited. The rest of us converged upon him. "It's ringin'," he said, looking at the group. "Hey, detective work ain't always pretty, huh?"

Wally and Earl's friend, Billy, an employee of the selective service system, said they would owe him a steak dinner and that it would be easier for him to go down to the office himself and call them with what came up on the screen from the computer databank on Raymond Harris. Wally gave him all we had and said we'd be waiting by the phone.

An hour later, Billy called back and told Wally that this wouldn't be as easy as he had thought. Several aspects of the file were confidential, and he had to decode them before getting the whole picture.

"Could be another hour," he said.

"We'll wait," Wally told him.

"I can tell you one thing about this Harris, Wally. He's not a good boy."

"You're not breakin' my heart, Billy. That's what we wanna hear."

By 11 P.M., we had each taken our turn waiting for the call while the rest strolled outside, lounged in chairs, visited Earl's apartment and mine, and fidgeted. The rest of us were chatting in the parking lot when Margo tapped on the window from upstairs, the phone to her ear.

We bounded up the stairs, Wally actually leading the way. "Yeah, Billy?" he said, gasping. "Let me put our secretary Bonnie on, and she can type it as you read it off. Thanks a million, pal."

Bonnie put the phone to her ear and rolled a piece of paper into the typewriter. Quickly she began tapping out:

Harris, Raymond (Ray) Albrecht, born 2 September 49, Hereford, Texas; raised, Umbarger, Texas; high school drop-out, spring 1967; selective service classification number 053; drafted September 1967; five foot, eleven inches, one hundred sixty-five pounds, eyes green, hair brown, no scars or distinguishing marks (note: see criminal record below); conscientious objector status denied, November 1967; denied entry to Canada, December 1967; charged with evading the draft, January 1968; overturned due to enlistment, January 1968; promoted from recruit to private, April 1968; assigned Vietnam, August 1968; promoted from private to private first class, August 1968, assigned to munitions/explosives detail; demoted to private, October

1968, charged with insubordination; demoted to recruit, November 1968, charged with threatening superior officer; reported AWOL, December 1968; apprehended in Cambodia and scheduled to return to U.S. for dishonorable discharge, February 1969; reported escaped from evac unit, February 1969, listed AWOL; apparently captured by Viet Cong, March 1969, listed as POW, Haiphong; status changed from AWOL to MIA/POW, to be reviewed upon return to unit; escaped POW camp, Haiphong, returned with injured left thigh (shrapnel) to unit, June 1969; evacuated to U.S. July 1969, Ft. Benning, Georgia; desertion charges overturned, September 1969; dishonorably discharged for other infractions; decoration for wound in the line of duty resulted in dishonorable discharge being overturned, January 1970; criminal record reported to SSS by local authorities, beginning March 1970 through September 1971; new scars and/or distinguishing characteristics; eight-inch shrapnel scar on right thigh, pronounced limp, unaccounted for scar on right side of forehead, approx. one-inch square; aliases: Ramie, Rays, Tim, Timmy, Beam, Beams; occupation: none; last known address: Route 2, Claphan, New Mexico; current status: despite honorable discharge, Harris considered persona non grata and guilty of conduct not suited to a veteran of the United States Armed Forces.

"Lemme have the horn, Bonnie. Hey, thanks, Billy. What do you make of the lack of a criminal record for more than ten years? . . . Oh yeah? We got another idea on that, but we'll get into it at dinner sometime, soon, huh pal? Well, awright!"

Wally hung up and turned to Earl. "He wants us to tell this guy, if we know who he is, that he can get his status changed by reporting his current address and occupation to the government. He says they don't hold grudges and would wipe all that civilian crime stuff out of the files if he's kept his nose clean since 1971. Is that a scream?"

While Freeman was trying to talk nurses at the vet hospital into letting him talk to Tim Bemis, Earl was calling Amos

Chakaris, former lawyer and former Illinois Secretary of State, to see who would be the best federal judge to contact in an effort to reopen the case.

"If you've got this much," Chakaris told Earl, "you may not have to go back into court at all. Lahr will be important and, of course, locating this Harris character will be your whole case. Who knows what identity he's using now? You've sure got his motive dead to rights. He never wanted to be in the service in the first place, so he blamed his draft board for everything that happened to him."

"I hope we don't need much from Bemis on this," Freeman reported. "He says he has a vague recollection of talking with a Texan in Haiphong, but all he remembers is the accent, no name, no history, no face."

"We won't need it," Earl said. "What we need is a criminal file on Harris, along with a photo or prints we can match to his service record. Then I want to see Mr. Lahr and Mr. Bemis reacquainted. I'll bet the Navy would finance that for us just to clear the name of one of their men."

"Is it really almost over?" Lindsey asked, hardly able to believe it.

"Almost," Earl said. "The problem is, if we don't find Harris, all we have is proof that Timothy didn't pull the jobs he was credited for in the Southwest, and we have someone else with a better motive for murdering Cavenaugh. By tomorrow Harris will be on the FBI wanted list, and his picture will be all over the country. He'd have to be a pretty good magician to hide from this manhunt. Congratulations, dear, you were right all along."

EPILOGUE

I'm anything but superstitious, but I'll bet Raymond A. Harris won't be walking under any ladders for a while. He was apprehended Friday the thirteenth of May, while trying to use another alias in Raton, New Mexico. As the statute of limitations does not apply to murder cases, Harris was arrested and scheduled to face federal charges within the month.

Timothy Bemis was released to the custody of his attorney, Harold Freeman, who was optimistic about the chances of getting several years of back pay from the Navy. The only hitch was the desertion charge still hanging over Bemis's head, but worse things had been forgiven since Vietnam.

An emotional highlight in all of our lives came the night we had dinner with Timothy and Lindsey and Harold, and then went to O'Hare to meet Chief Petty Officer Kenneth Lahr. He was in uniform and easy to spot, but of course he didn't recognize Tim.

They went before a federal judge, who took a deposition from Lahr and shook hands with both men. Tim approached Lahr and threw his arms around him. "This is the second time I've grabbed you," he said, fighting tears. "And the second time you've saved my life."

Freeman was also busy on Wally's squabble with the police department, which we all selfishly hoped would result in

Wally's taking over the agency for Earl. We wouldn't know for several weeks.

We got the impression that Harold was also busy on Lindsey's case, if you know what I mean.

Our wedding day was so stereotypical that we could have been disappointed if we hadn't been so happy.

I was the nervous groom, hardly sleeping the night before, panicky because I thought I'd forget everything, including my vows, which I didn't. Talk about your typical beautiful bride. Well, I don't know about typical, but Margo was radiant.

I stood there at the front of the church, trying to hold back my tears, and I could see all the people who had meant so much to us over the years.

Wally had tried to relax a minute by sitting while his tux was buttoned. He looked as if he were about to burst or float to the ceiling, one of the two. Well, the former happened, and now as he stood up front with Earl, Larry, a couple of friends from church, and me, he kept trying to hold his coat closed.

My mother, whom I hadn't seen since before I met Margo, had fallen in love with my bride by mail and had begun crying before the usher got her to her seat. Dad, proud but embarrassed and always uncomfortable when he had to sit long, sat grinning, trying to pretend he was doing more than just enduring.

The girls came down the aisle, each in a dress she had made herself and looking as if she were about to die of fright. All, that is, except Bonnie's granddaughter, Erin, who was an internationally ranked gymnast and was used to crowds.

Bonnie herself made it up to the foyer when she heard the wedding march and stood there dabbing her eyes with one hand and licking the fingers of the other.

I knew I'd be nervous and emotional, but I can't describe the feeling I had when Margo appeared at the back on her father's arm. I lost sight of everything and everyone else. It was as if I had no peripheral vision. I caught her eye, and we locked in on each other during the whole, slow walk to the front. About halfway down the aisle, she flashed me a huge smile, the one I thought I had gotten used to, the one that used to make me catch my breath. It was working again.

Her hair was done differently than it had been in the morning, falling down the left side of her face. I had not seen her dress before. She had kept it carefully hidden during fittings and photographs for the newspaper. What a delicious surprise. For a second I wished I had a camera, and then I knew that I would never forget that vision. I loved her with all that was in me, and I tried to tell her with my look. She was loving me, too.

I had feared the panic that would make me want to turn tail and run when everything started closing in, but it never even crossed my mind. This was so right, so perfect, so beautifully timed. We hadn't been ready the first time around; we had needed to grow.

"Who gives this woman to be married to this man?"

"I do."

Mr. Franklin lifted her veil and pecked her on the cheek.

Our favorite songs were played and sung. The pastor spoke about the sanctity of marriage and compared it to Christ and His bride, the church. We exchanged rings, had songs sung to each other by soloists, and then recited our vows.

"Philip, I take you to be my husband because God has brought us together and willed it. I love you, and I will cherish you and be yours forever through bad times and good, sickness and health, poverty or wealth. I will keep you only unto myself for as long as we both shall live, or until Christ, who has saved us by His grace, returns to take us unto Himself forever.

"When we met, you showed me a life-saving love that led

me to my Savior. For that I will be eternally grateful and will live my life with you and for you in thanks for that gift. And when we fell in love, you showed me fulfilling love that I will want to give back for as long as I have breath. I love you, and I am yours, and we are Christ's."

I could hardly speak. I had read Margo's vows. I had heard her run through them at the rehearsal. Yet to hear them now, so sweet and sincere and lovely, I would rather have cried than speak. But I wanted to pledge my love to her, too. Just before the pastor prompted me, I began:

"Margo, I take you to be my wife because God has brought us together and willed it. I love you, and I will cherish you and be yours forever through bad times and good, sickness and health, poverty or wealth. I will keep you only unto myself for as long as we both shall live, or until Christ, who has saved us by His grace, returns to take us unto Himself forever.

"When we met, you needed more than I had to give, and I directed you to the only source I knew.

"You responded to the love of God, and when our dependence upon each other—born of trauma—turned to love, you responded to mine and gave me more than I could ever hope to give you. My wish is to live my life with you and for you in thanks for that gift. I want to return your inspiring love for as long as I have breath. I love you, and I am yours, and we are Christ's."

"And now by the power vested in me by the state of Illinois and as a minister of the Gospel of Jesus Christ, I pronounce you husband and wife. You may kiss the bride."

And I did.

"Ladies and gentlemen, may I introduce Mr. and Mrs. Philip Spence." Where we went on our honeymoon was a secret. It still is.

an
He
w
B

b
L
C

hies
Orel
nine
yton,
Clary.
igious
ader's
major

ly and
Kalama-
with his
and Mi-